SUPPOSE

By

D. J. ADAMSON

ISBN: 979-8-9886593-3-4

Published 2014

Printing   3 4 5 6 7 8 9

Also By

Forever Loved and Missed,
Patricia

CHAPTER ONE
OCTOBER 29TH   A CRIME COMITTED

R eal things started happening. No more ducking my head. No more playing the blame game. That's the problem with being sober and taking life on without a drink in my hand. Don't get me wrong. My drinking is not an excuse for who I'm not. But my NOT drinking is the only way I'll find out who I was before taking that first drink.

It was time for me to start doing sober what I always said I'd do drunk.

All eyes were on me; mine are wide

I own the AAA Discount Liquor store in Frytown, Iowa. Called Discount by the locals, it has the lowest prices this side of Walmart. Most folks go to the Hy-Vee grocery for their wine and beer, but for the harder booze, they come here.

I inherited the store from Clarence Saltzman, who passed away last August from a complication of the flu. Yes, the flu can kill. I wasn't sure why he named me as his beneficiary. Others in Frytown probably wondered the same.

One thing about a small town, if people have time on their hands, they stray into someone else's business.

If they knew I was a recovering alcoholic, tongues would definitely wag. But so far, it's been my little secret.

An alchie owning a liquor store?

Life has its ironies.

Discount has regulars like Mrs. Atkins, who comes in every third Wednesday of the month to buy her bottle of Apricot Brandy and her husband's bottle of sherry. Even though I've never asked, Mrs. Atkins once told me she and her husband have a drink every evening when they sit down to watch the evening news.

"One drink and never more than one," she emphasized. "It's good for our digestion."

I've had an ingestion of alcohol since I was twelve.

Today I'm five years sober.

Today, not tomorrow.

Tomorrow may never arrive.

Mrs. Atkins didn't come into the store this Wednesday for her usual order, and that gave me suspect something might be wrong. After closing the store, I headed to their house on the corner of Maple and Third. The house mirrored their conservative values: white siding, blue shutters, red, cheery front door, and a white picket fence. Showy, but not a spit in the face, I've done better than you kind of house. Mr. Atkins was a retired professor from the University of Iowa, and Mrs. Atkins once held the revered position as president of the Frytown Women's Club.

The Atkins weighed on a much higher social scale than I. I wasted most of my youth balancing on a bar stool in a class B cocktail lounge.

I was still a lightweight. At thirty-six, I lived in a Senior Residential Condominium Complex called Lake View.

However, since coming to Frytown, my life had slightly elevated. Two things uplifted me to see myself and my life differently: sobriety and owning my own business. If I lost what I've achieved, well, I'm not sure what I would become.

As soon as Mrs. Atkins opened the door, I realized she wasn't her usual self. Her creamy-white, always-wear-a-bonnet complexion appeared more like her bonnet had been blown away. Her hair was generally pulled neatly in tortoiseshell combs, and she'd haphazardly fixed back with bobby pins. She blinked and shaded her eyes from the sudden brightness. "Lillian? What brings you here?"

"It's Wednesday?" It was less than a thorough explanation, so I added, "Discount?"

"What time is it?"

"After six."

"Good grief. Have we been sitting in front of that television all day?" It was both a question and a statement. She pulled the door wider. "Come in. Come in." She announced me. "Paul. We've got company."

"I don't want to bother you." I stepped inside and stood waiting, unsure of what to do next. I hadn't thought to bring their order with me. The store doesn't offer a delivery service.

"Don't be silly. You're not bothering us." She shut the door. "Come in." She led me into the living room, where Mr. Atkins sat in his recliner. His COPD machine was conveniently set on a small table next to his chair, where he was sucking on the receptacle, replacing two packs a day he'd shoved between his lips before his heart attack. Seeing me, he grabbed the television remote off the table and lowered the volume. "What brings you here, Lillian?"

I was about to explain again the significance of it being Wednesday when his head jerked back to the television. He increased the volume, and waved, "Sit down. Sit down."

As required, I took a seat on the sofa. Mrs. Atkins followed by slipping into her gliding rocker. On the TV was Bobby Bowen of the KETV News Channel.

"We are waiting for Mayor Otis Johns, mayor of the City of Frytown, to comment on today's astounding declaration by Ms. Jessica Feldman that she has been married to the mayor for the last three years. Living in Baxter, a small city outside of Davenport, she declares she was not aware Mr. Johns was the mayor of Frytown, or that he celebrated his forty-fifth wedding anniversary with his wife this past January, two months before she succumbed to cancer."

Bowen was standing in front of City Hall, where reporters and a crowd had gathered. A podium was positioned with microphones. "This declaration came as a shock to the citizens of Frytown, who knew the mayor's wife. The incident also comes at a critical moment for a city deciding whether to re-elect their mayor for his seventh term in office."

He paused to let his audience catch up, and then asked, "Will the announcement Ms. Feldman made today unseat Frytown's mayor for re-election? Is Mayor Otis Johns an alleged bigamist?"

Bobby Bowen slicked back his hair with his free hand before pushing the sleeves of his mock-turtle-neck sweater past his elbows. The doors of City Hall opened, and two people descended the steps. Bowen identified the older of the two as Councilman Andrew Pane. The other, is the mayor's son, Jim Johns.

Jim took the microphone. A drawn face with dark circles under his eyes gave away he'd had a bad night's sleep. He pulled a folded piece of paper from his shirt pocket. His voice tendered in saying, "As you can guess, my father is very distraught by this woman's accusation, especially since my mother passed away only a few months ago from a long, disabling illness. My father," his voice caught in his throat. He amended, "Our family, misses my mother very much, and we are all still grieving her loss."

He turned to the note in his hand and read: "Mayor Johns does not know Jessica Feldman, nor has he had any relationship with her. He asks all of Frytown to pray for her." He folded and restored the formal announcement back in his pocket.

Out of the corner of my eye, I saw Mrs. Atkins in her rocker nodding in agreement. If I recalled correctly, the Johns and the Atkins were both members of St. Mark's Episcopal Church.

Before Jim Johns could catch his breath, the news media began firing questions. "Is your father saying he never met Jessica Feldman?"

Jim squared his shoulders. "My father meets a great many people. What I am saying." He corrected himself, "What he is saying is that he has never had a sexual relationship with this woman or any other woman other than my mother." His neck slightly reddened as if embarrassed by the remark.

"He doesn't recollect having met her, however, a man in his position meets a great many people. They could have generally met in passing."

Mrs. Atkins asked, "Why would a young woman be interested in Otis Johns? For land's sake, Otis is in his sixties. They say this woman is somewhere in her thirties."

Mr. Atkins gave a one-word answer, "Money." Then he shushed us again.

"Mr. Johns? KETV. The mayor says he wants us to pray for her. Can you tell the viewers why a woman such as Ms. Feldman would come out publicly if she'd never met your father?"

"I'm telling you," Mr. Atkins shouted as if Bowen asked him. "Money."

Mrs. Atkins hushed him. "Otis hasn't much more money than you or me, Paul."

He shot back, "Then maybe there's still a chance for me." He looked over at me and winked. "Think I could still lead a young woman your age astray?"

I returned the wink. But before I had a chance to gratify him with a witty reply, his wife did. "Maybe we'll put an ad in personals and see if we get any takers."

Mr. Atkins scowled and gave me another wink.

Councilman Pane walked over to stand by Jim. Pane was the owner of the Dairy Queen and two other fast-food restaurants in town. Actually, he owned the only fast-food restaurants in Frytown, thus making himself his only competitor.

"Like I said, he has never met the woman." Jim pivoted on his heel and walked confidently back toward City Hall.

"Mr. Johns?" Bowen started after him. "What if I tell you Ms. Feldman says she's willing to produce a marriage license with your father's signature?"

Jim halted and whipped around. "She's lying."

"What about you?" Bowen asked. "Do YOU know Jessica Feldman?"

Jim startled, a deer caught in headlights, suddenly seeming indecisive about whether to go back or continue. He glanced at the podium where Councilman Pane remained standing. He gave a look ahead at City Hall. Then he moved off to the safer of the two.

The camera found Bowen back at the podium where Councilman Pane stood answering questions. Bowen asked, "Can you tell us when the mayor learned of Ms. Feldman's accusation and when he notified the City Council?"

The councilman cleared his throat. "That's all the time we have for questions. The mayor will personally give a public statement tomorrow morning."

But Bowen seemed unstoppable. "Is the mayor considering pulling out of the campaign?"

This question got an angry, one-word response. "No."

Bowen tried again. "Has Ms. Feldman contacted the mayor or any of his family directly?"

"No." The councilman pursed his lips and glowered. "There is no reason for the mayor to lie to the citizens of Frytown." He addressed the crowd. "I will take no more questions. You will hear next from the mayor himself."

Again, Bowen wasn't so easily thwarted. "Is the mayor willing to come on my show and end all of our confusion?"

Councilman Pane's eyes fluttered and shifted around the grouping. His lips parted as if he was about to answer, then he shut his mouth and motioned to someone beyond the crowd to come forward. Lieutenant Manville of the Frytown Police Force walked within the camera's range. The two men exchanged words. Then Councilman Pane took the same path a Jim Johns.

Lieutenant Manville raised his hands, waiting for the crowd standing before him to quiet. "That's it, folks. As the councilman said, the mayor will make another statement tomorrow." But reporters continued throwing detailed questions. "Is Ms. Feldman filing criminal charges? Has Chief Kaefring spoken with her? Will the mayor be arrested for bigamy?"

"No comment." The lieutenant answered.

Then a faint voice pulled above all voices as the crowd quieted. "What does the mayor have to say about family values now?"

Cameras spun for the woman's voice but alighted on no one taking responsibility for the comment.

Mr. Atkins flicked off the set with the remote.

Mrs. Atkins asked, "Who do you suppose shouted that?"

"Someone voting for Morton Dyer," Mr. Atkins quipped.

"Well, I know for a fact Otis was devoted to Corabelle. He never left her bedside. Not in all the days she was sick."

"A total exaggeration. The man had to eat and work."

"Oh, you know what I mean. Don't be so contrary."

Mr. Atkins switched on his Breathalyzer. "If there's a grain of truth in any of it, it'll cost him the election."

"Phooey." Mrs. Atkins waved away his speculation.

She walked me to the front door. "I miss Clarence each time I step into the store, Lillian, but it's always nice to see you behind the counter." She grasped my arm, giving it a slight squeeze. "Thank you for worrying about us."

"I can always deliver if you need."

"I like getting out. Besides, Paul's cutting back."

Overhearing us, Mr. Atkins called out. "First, my cigarettes. Now my sherry. I've got this to live for." Glancing over Mrs. Atkin's shoulder, I saw him shaking his mouthpiece at us. He grinned and winked, calling out, "Pretty soon, she'll be collecting on my life insurance policy."

The comment didn't seem to bother her. "You don't have any life insurance, Paul, so if you're figuring to call it quits and dying anytime soon, let me know so I can get some." She whispered covertly to me, "His blood pressure is much better."

We both stood in the open doorway. Looking outside, she shivered. "Getting colder. They say we'll have snow before Thanksgiving."

I wrapped my arms around myself, giving a shiver, too.

CHAPTER TWO

Bacardi sat in the kitchen doorway, waiting for my arrival. He gave a giant yowl and padded off in the direction of his complaint.

Bacardi's coloring, brown and yellow, reminded me of my teenage penchant for rum and coke. His hair fizzing out from his body gave him a cartoonish appearance as if he'd stuck his claw into a light socket, and his face appeared smashed as if hit by a hammer. When people first meet him, they wonder what attracted me to him. I don't bother explaining how I've woken a time or two after a hard night of drinking and saw something relatively similar in the mirror.

I pulled a can of Feline Delight from the cupboard, scooped food into his dish, then refilled his kibble, and refreshed his water. With him fed, I pulled the last two pieces of bread out of the bag, checked for mold, grabbed the peanut butter jar, and started spreading. I added a wilted but still edible piece of lettuce for my veggie, and reasoned jam would satisfy any fruit requirement.

I headed to switch on the TV. If Mr. and Mrs. Atkins had been watching the news most of the day, I might have missed something. The mayor was definitely in a pickle. In a small town, a personal taint can hang around someone's neck whether they're guilty or not.

Passing my desk where I kept my computer and handled Discount's accounting, the answering machine's light signaled messages:

Green for Good.

Red for "STOP!" Your day is about to be ruined.

"You have three new messages."

A cold draft of regret instantly moved over me.

Marilyn Yoder's voice came over the machine. Marilyn manages Oaks Manor Convalescent Hospital, where my mother, Dahlia, lives. Her tone was breezy as if delivering good news. "The doctor saw your mother this morning. He gave her a good report. Your mother said…" I hit the erase button.

My brother Frank dumped Dahlia on me, causing me to have to move to Frytown into her senior condo. If he would have left a forwarding address or his telephone number, I'd leave a few messages on his machine. He swore she didn't have long to live. That was five years ago.

I took an angry bite out of my sandwich.

The next message was from Donna Stockman, Frytown's Gossipedia, and first-shift dispatch operator for the Frytown Police. "I've been trying to reach you. Turn on the television."

Again I hit the erase button. Shfrome was calling about the mayor's commotion. I'd call her back later.

I took another bite and frowned seeing jam had dribbled on my white blouse. I was hoping to get another day out of it.

The third voice startled me. My mouth fell open in horror.

"Hello, Lillian. It's me, Kenny."

Kenny Liky: Easy on the eyes. A Johnny Depp, Ryan Seacrest, André Aggosi type. Maybe Brad Pitt would be a better example. That is if you remembered the movie *Interview with a Vampire*. Because Kenny could suck your blood dry in one guzzle without you thinking you'd been pricked by anything more than a mosquito.

My finger was about to press the "Don't Give a Rat's Ass" button, when he said as if he could see me, "Don't erase this message. You'll want to hear me out."

No, wrong. I never wanted to hear from him.

"I'm dying."

On second thought, maybe messages do bring good news.

"I've only got a couple of weeks, maybe not that long."

Yeah, sure. A con artist and a chronic gambler, he ate Oxytocin as if they were M&M's. Was he high?

Kenny lived with my friend Cressie. He'd discovered her dead in their apartment. Dead from an alcohol and barbiturate overdose. Dead, after she'd been clean and sober for eight years. Her death never made sense to me. Cressie was hell-bent on staying sober.

But she wouldn't be the first alcoholic to slip and slide back into the bottle. Her dying inspired my sobriety. For the first time, I clearly saw how my proclivity for wallowing in misery was no recipe for living happily ever after. Or making it much past the ripe ol'age of forty.

But pills? She hated Kenny's addiction to narcotics and mentioned more than once how the threat to their relationship wasn't his conning or gambling, but his penchant for popping and selling Oxy.

I stood with my index finger hovering over the erase button.

"I found her camera."

At first, I had no idea what he was talking about. Then I knew exactly what he'd found. She'd suspected he was dealing out of their apartment. She'd come across some female intimates that weren't hers. He denied it, of course. Could Kenny ever tell the truth? When she confided in me, I suggested she get a nanny cam so she could catch him in the act.

As I said, Kenny was scum, and Cressie deserved better. Especially when she was working so hard to beat off her own demons.

My finger felt the smooth surface of the button.

But I didn't push down fast enough.

"I got proof. You killed her."

CHAPTER THREE

A bell rung can't be unrung.

And an erase button left unused cannot be ignored.

I punched the callback button. The line rang, and when someone picked up, I didn't wait to make sure it was him. "Call me again, and I'm calling the police."

"Hey, Lillian." He gave a snigger. "How're you doin?"

"How dare you make such an allegation? Cressie was my friend. If anyone's responsible for her death, it's you."

"Tell you what. I can make all of this go away."

"I can do that without your help. I'm hanging up."

"Better not," his voice riddled. "The video I have puts you in a very compromising situation."

"You know why I don't believe you? Because I know when your lips are moving, whatever they're saying isn't true."

"Ah, now. Don't be like that. I'm calling to help you. As a friend. A hundred could make me throw this video away."

"Dollars?" I laughed and started to hang up, but he began chortling like someone off their meds.

"Not a hundred dollars. A hundred thousand."

Don't listen. Don't get caught up in his idiotic schemes, I warned myself. All you need to do is put the phone down. He's not dying. And he has nothing he can hurt you with. Erase his message. Forget he called.

He said, "I know you and Cressie were friends. Whatever happened had to have been an accident. Maybe the two of you began drinking together. Maybe you decided to sample some of my wares. Whatever. A jury will see her death as an accident. I'd bet on it."

He didn't take a breath. "Let me help you. I'll offer this as a gift because I loved Cressie. Give me what you can, and not only will I give you this flash drive, but I'll throw in the original memory card. No one'll be wiser."

I swallowed the bile rising in my throat. He had to be desperate to think I was going to buy this con he was selling. A hundred thousand dollars? He wasn't just an idiot. He was insane.

"Let me try to say this so you can understand," I returned with a firm direct menace uttered in each word. "You have nothing on me. I don't have any money. You've fried your brain. You've taken the yellow brick road to Looney Ville. Call here again and I'll call the Davenport Police. You've probably got a warrant out for your arrest. Is that it, Kenny? You're running from the police and need a little traveling money?"

He hooted as if I'd thrown out a joke. "And don't think I haven't heard how you're some big business woman."

How did he hear? I'd left no friends in Davenport. I'd split without leaving a forwarding address. Something my brother Frank and I have in common. Take off and leave no breadcrumb trail.

"You've got twenty-four hours. Give me what money you can. After all, we're old friends. But...if I don't see any money by then, what I have goes to the police." He sounded so damn sure of himself.

Kenny once conned a homeless person into giving him the last of his spare change. He told the guy he was going to the casino, and he'd play it on a craps' line, bring him back twice the amount in a couple of hours.

Slow down, I willed myself. Think this out. He must have something, but what? Had he concocted a video? Could something like that be faked? Sure. Weren't kids doing it all the time, putting stuff up on Facebook or YouTube? But did Kenny have those talents? I thought not. But if he talked someone into doing it for him, fake or not, he could screw up the new life I'd earned in Frytown.

If he gave the video to the Davenport Police, I'd be investigated. Frytown Police would be contacted. Gossip would mushroom.

Taint, taint, taint.

Damn.

I offered. "I want to see what you're holding, first, then we'll talk money."

"We can arrange that. But, no tricks. Remember, I've got the memory card."

"You're the con, Kenny, not me."

"Okay. You drive a hard bargain. Maybe that's because you own a business. You weren't so sophisticated in the past. Let's meet at the River Casino. Tomorrow night, in the bar at six. Maybe I'll buy you a drink. We can talk about old times."

The suggestion told me Kenny didn't know everything about the new me. Nevertheless, he knew about Discount.

I scribbled down the telephone number he was calling from in case I needed it later. "No thanks. Just show me the video."

Then I did what I should have done three minutes earlier.

I pushed ERASE.

CHAPTER FOUR

F eeling a bit befuddled, I left the pb&j on the desk and moved into the living room to switch on the TV. I needed to replace Kenny's voice with something, anything else.

An anchor for KETV was saying, "A charge of bigamy is a serious matter, Pamela."

"You can say that again, Bill." The co-anchor took the camera. "If this alleged incident is real, the mayor of Frytown could be sentenced to a year in prison and fined."

Why would the mayor have an affair while his wife was dying of cancer? Could a marriage license be faked? If this woman was blackmailing the mayor with a fake license, then Kenny could have made a video making it look like I had something to do with Cressie's death.

But why me? And again, who told him I had a business? I thought through all the people I knew in Frytown. Where was the connection? I had been on the Bobby Bowen show when I became an eyewitness for the arson fire, but I didn't own the store then. Had a reporter mentioned the store in a newspaper article? Did Kenny read a newspaper? Could he read?

Okay, he wasn't exactly illiterate. But he didn't show off an intellectual side. He was even bad at gambling and conning.

He thinks I have money because I have a business. Is that what the woman is after with the mayor? Money? Mr. Atkins thought so. But why go public? Why was she going on the Bobby Bowen show? Her agreement begged the question of her legitimacy.

My meeting with Kenny didn't mean I thought his blackmail was legitimate. But, undoubtedly, he'd heard rumors. Maybe someone saw the Bowen show and told him about me and Discount. Someone connected me then as the owner. Who? Still, having a liquor store doesn't mean I'm flush. Although, I'm not exactly broke.

Yet, if anything happened, I'd be back in the soup line. Fast!

Bill responded to Pamela, mentioning a fine. "The fifteen hundred dollars the state gets is a drop-in-the-bucket to what a civil lawsuit could mean."

Civil lawsuit. If I remember correctly, a civil lawsuit only requires a reasonable doubt. A young woman betrayed by an older man, shown to be immoral by having an affair while his wife was dying, would sway an audience. My bet was the woman was looking for a settlement, and the mayor's lawyers might give it to her to get her to move back into the shadows.

The mayor could have met her in a hotel. They could have had a drink together. Cons aren't gender-specific. There are a lot of greedy people out there thinking they're owed more than life gave them.

I guess I think that way, too. But I don't plan to hurt anyone. And I'm working backward. Moving from a miserable lifestyle to becoming a better person.

I've failed at a lot of things in my life, but this time, I wanted to be a winner.

The police and lawyers will get this woman sorted out.

Hold it. Kenny said a hundred, but he'd take fifty bucks. I was sure of it. Only, if I gave in and gave him anything, he'd only be back for more.

And at the time, the police said Cressie's death was a suicide. So if Kenny did take the video to them, they wouldn't give him the time of day. It's been five years. Why would they remember the death of another OD found alone in an apartment? The coroner must get a call a week with just that description.

The mayor's situation was entirely different. It was fresh. A new story. The press was all over it.

"Not to mention losing his seat as mayor." Pamela turned to Bobby Bowen, sitting just off-camera next to her. Bowen took the lead. "Many are holding off judgment until Mayor Johns' press conference tomorrow morning." He paused. Then added, "But even if the mayor again denies these allegations, viewers will want to hear from Jessica Feldman. Tune in to my show, Iowa's History, and Its People."

"Friday night," Peggy chimed in, camera returning to her.

I punched off the set. I didn't need to hear anymore. Bigamist was being chiseled onto the mayor's epitaph. Even if proven not guilty, there would be those who would always wonder if there'd been some truth to it. I'd suffer the same if I let Kenny get out of hand.

I had no other choice. I had to go back to Davenport and deal with Kenny.

I passed Bacardi lying on the carpet on his back, legs limp and tail popping, dreaming. One big, happy kitty, relaxed after a bowlful of Feline Delight. My peanut butter sandwich lay like a lump of lead in my stomach. I picked up the pb&j off the desk and tossed it in the trashcan. Then I picked up the phone and returned Donna's call. It went through to her voice mail, meaning I was in a line of callers wanting to get "the latest."

"I got your message, Donna. I've been keeping up with the mayor's trouble. It's pretty hard to believe. I'll check back with you later. I'm sure you've got the low down on what this woman's up to."

If anyone did, it'd be Donna. When I talked to her, maybe she'd suggest someone who could take care of the store for a day.

One day. Just one day, twenty-four hours out of a lifetime. If my going stopped Kenny before he leered me into whatever scheme he was playing, then the trip to Davenport would be well worth the time and trouble.

It was almost eight o'clock. By routine, I usually stopped by Oaks Manor to check on Dahlia, but tonight I'd gone straight to the Atkins. I'd been tired and wanted to come home and relax.

Right. That didn't happen. I hadn't stopped talking to myself since I heard Kenny's message. Pretty soon, I'd be answering myself, too.

Okay, so I've been answering myself. But who else do I have to talk to other than Bacardi?

I considered the consequences of my going or not. Missing a night didn't ping my daughter-guilt. Dahlia and I've never been exactly close. The thought, however, of not making a show generated a sense of dread. This night hadn't started off well. Getting the call from Kenny was a bad omen. Missing a night with Dahlia would be as ominous. She'd fester up another fiasco to make my life troublesome if I didn't come by. She'd make trouble at Oaks. Be meaner than normal to her nurse or other residents. Or find a way to personally penalize me. Dahlia's world was always about Dahlia. Her tit-for-tat in my not showing up could be bruising. Oaks would call, wanting me to keep her in line. As if that was possible and I had such power. They'd say the nurse was threatening to quit again, and they were running out of nurses. Frytown is not a medical Mecca for nursing personnel. This was about the eighth or ninth nurse scheduled on her corridor.

To get and keep this new life, I realized last summer that I couldn't let Dahlia die. Not yet. I needed to figure out how the child in me became so lost. How I'd become so fractured. Twelve-year-olds don't live their childhoods becoming drunks. It's not normal.

My father was an alcoholic. No, he never abused me. He never asked to have anyone pick him off the front lawn and drag him inside the house into bed. That was all Dahlia.

She was the abuser. No matter the hour, she woke me to help her rescue him from the neighbors' prying eyes and flapping tongues.

My scars from her neglect still bleed.

No matter what, I have to keep her living. A haunting, recurring dream continues to point to her as the key.

Davenport. I needed a vacation. I could give myself a mini-vacation. Stay over after showing Kenny where he could put his flash drive and memory card. The thought of a hotel room, dinner, and time to read a book was enticing. *Me* time.

The thought of getting away from everything gave me enough resolve to get back in the car and head to Oaks Manor. After Kenny's call, adding Dahlia to the night's agenda couldn't make the evening any worse.

CHAPTER FIVE

I f someone led me into Oaks Manor Convalescent Home blindfolded, I'd instantly know where I was. There's no mistaking the underlying aromas of urine, unwashed bodies, and Wednesday night's Meat Loaf special.

"Ahoy there, Matey." RN Nelly Crow stood behind the reception counter wearing a black pirate's scarf, a large gold earring, and an eye patch over her left eye.

Halloween's not until Friday," I returned, and asked, "Are you allowed to celebrate Halloween?"

Nelly's a Mennonite, and while the Mennonites aren't as strict as the Amish, I didn't think they were allowed to celebrate a holiday where evil spirits might be roaming.

"Conservative orders don't," she said, taking the small plastic sword she held and scratching her head beneath the scarf. I caught a glimpse of her white, netted cap, worn still by many of the Mennonite women. "But our church is celebrating Harvest Day and Halloween together, so the kids don't feel left out." She brandished her sword. "Take that, and that." She laughed. "We needed to have some early fun here at the home. Get everyone in a good mood." She gave another playful stab, "Take that, you devil."

"Very liberal."

"Don't forget Jesus walked among the multitudes."

"What are you doing here so late?" Nelly generally worked the day shift.

"Mary Niles needed the night off. Stover's mother's in town visiting."

I glanced around. "Is Dahlia watching TV or in her room?"

"I think she's in her room."

I moved in that direction.

Nelly called, "You know the doctor gave her a good report this morning?"

"I heard."

She added in her pirate voice, "Be careful, me Matey, there're monsters and goblins around in these halls." She laughed. "Don't miss seeing Buster Smith. He's dressed in a diaper and carrying a huge baby bottle."

Buster Smith was over two hundred pounds and hairy. Seeing him in a diaper was something I could miss.

I found Dahlia lying on her bed. Her eyes were closed. She appeared so innocent. Frail. She opened her eyes, saw me, and said. "Where the hell have you been?"

I heaved a sigh. Frail? Not my mother.

"I told you, Dahlia. I may not be able to come every night anymore. I have got a store to run."

When I'd told her I inherited the store, she'd said, "How'd you wiggle that out of HIM?" I was expecting more of the same, but she said sprightly, "I saw the doctor today."

Her not taking advantage of an opening for a well-aimed shot put me on guard. I went over to her closet, making busy with her laundry.

The doctor had been keeping a close eye on Dahlia after she almost died from poisoning last August. An event she still blamed on me. "If you'd keep your nose out of other people's business." Having come across a house fire and called it into Dispatch, I became an eyewitness to arson, causing me to be hunted down by the arsonist and a man from Dahlia's past, who threatened to kill us both.

Last summer, seeing her in a hospital bed with machines beeping her existence, the little girl in me awoke. A Lillian I'd buried saw not Dahlia but her mommy.

She was so sick. So close to death.

My mother was never sick. Nothing ever struck my mother down. And yet, lying in the bed was a mommy, pale and vulnerable.

My inner child shook to my infantile core.

I shook that little girl back into oblivion. I chalked the relapse to the telescoping vision of having a flash of my mortality. Life doesn't last forever.

"Lillian. Did you hear me?"

"I heard the doctor gave you a thumb's up."

You're under my thumb Dahlia, I mused. Not the other way around. You have no more control over me.

Oaks Manor laundered the bedding and would also have cleaned her clothing, but Dahlia never accepted hand-me-downs, and the Dove family never had much to give to charity. She provided for hers, and she expected others to do the same.

Nor did she tolerate stealing. The one time I lifted some nail polish-- "Can't afford fripperies"-- she made me return it. She apologized for having raised a criminal.

When we arrived home, she handed me a can of paint and a brush and told me to go out and paint the fence. If I had such an overwhelming desire to paint something, it might as well be something useful.

The fence ran from both sides of our house to the street, separating us from our neighbors. I wasn't allowed back inside until it was done. My brothers, Frankie and Patrick watched from the window.

The one time Dahlia saw one of her blouses worn by someone--accidentally hung in the wrong closet--she took off in her wheelchair chasing after the poor woman, threatening to run her over, then, "Rip MY SHIRT off your back."

Oaks Manor was pretty good at putting up with Dahlia's sour attitude, but at that unexpected incident, they warned me such aggressive behavior might make her residential arrangement problematic.

I'd told Dahlia she couldn't chase other residents like a madwoman. She took the counsel to heart. She hadn't pursued anyone else, to my knowledge, but she continued to speak her mind, and several times she'd taken off on her own, without prior permission.

"Lillian? Pay attention."

"I've heard every word," I told her. "I already knew what the doctor said. Marilyn called me."

Can't do anything without my knowing, Dahlia.

"Marilyn Yoder can mind her own business," she snapped. "If I want you to know something, I'll tell you."

She sat up. Smoothed out her covers.

No one ever called Dahlia a small woman. Her shoulders rounded and stooped slightly from working two jobs, one at a window factory, and a second, graveyard shift at Jimmy Dean's Foods. In her prime, even if Dahlia came home dead tired, she could pick each of my brothers up under her arms, kick my butt, and fold the laundry, all at the same time.

Thinking I had any control or leverage over her was an absolute pipedream.

"He says I'm as good as new."

They'd recently permed her white curls. Her cheeks glowed pink with her better health. She smiled innocently.

I repeated. "Good to hear." Duty finished, I glanced from her to the open doorway. Time to go.

"So, guess what I've decided?"

She asked like a young girl would, who'd worried and fretted and finally came to the determination that yes, indeed, she'd let her boyfriend give her a kiss.

I tugged at my shirt collar. Dahlia wasn't a young girl. Her question was leading to something far more worrying than an innocent kiss.

Bad luck was latching itself onto me like a bad cold.

The room narrowed. I couldn't breathe. I needed to get out before whatever she was building to, exploded.

I took a couple of steps to the doorway, hoping to find Buster. I needed a diversion. A hairy man wearing a diaper would be a welcomed digression.

"He says I can go home."

"What?" I whipped around. "What do you mean he said you could go home? You *are* home."

She smiled as big as a hungry cat, having eyed a slow, pudgy mouse. "He said I was as good as new. So, you need to move out. I'm moving back in."

Surely the doctor hadn't suggested she was well enough to leave Oaks Manor? He couldn't have. He wouldn't have.

Right?

"He may have said you're doing well. And you are. You recovered from almost dying."

"No thanks to you."

I burned. She wasn't listening. "I had nothing to do with Edgar Pike. He was *your* old boyfriend."

My comeback hit hard. Her eyes pulled away to something on the wall next to her. Her lips worrying.

But if I could hear the whine in my words, *It wasn't my fault, mommy*, then I was sure she'd heard them, too. Her hearing was age-impaired unless something was said not meant for her to catch.

I softened my voice, not wanting this to turn into a battle. "The doctor didn't mean you could live by yourself."

Her eyes came back to mine. Her gaze steadied. Her chin set. "Pack your stuff and get out."

The hair on my arms rose. Sweat broke on my upper lip.

"Look, I'll get the doctor to come back tomorrow. If the doctor says it's all right for you to move back to the condo and live by yourself, well, he's the expert."

I twisted around and headed for the corridor.

"I'm moving in. Do you hear me, Lillian June Dove? I don't care what that doctor says. You best get used to the idea."

"You need to call Marilyn," I said to Nelly on my way to the front doors. My tone posed more anger than Nelly deserved. After all, she couldn't control Dahlia, either. No one could.

"What's wrong?" She lifted her eye patch as if it was keeping her from understanding.

I stopped. "Tell Marilyn to get that doctor back," I warned. "Dahlia thinks she's well enough to go home. She says she's moving back into the condo."

"Oh my," Nelly cried. She started chewing on her sword.

CHAPTER SIX

The phone was ringing when I unlocked the door. I more than hesitated. Kenny, again? Dahlia? I answered it with the faint hope that Nelly hadn't bothered Marilyn and made an emergency call to the doctor. I hoped she was calling to tell me he was running right over to close the Pandora's box he'd opened.

Dahlia might not listen to me, but she would respect the doctor. Wouldn't she?

"Have you been keepin' up, Sweetie?' Donna's voice. "Mayor Otis has got his big toe into trouble." Her southern roots shined with Sweeties, Darlin's, and Hons.

"Allegedly," I reminded her.

I was more than happy to cast Dahlia out of my thoughts.

I took a deep breath, and let the steam all out. Forced my crazy brain to stop all the bad scenarios. By the time I returned, the doctor will have amended his words. Marilyn will have explained to Dahlia that returning to the condo wasn't a possibility. Of course, I wouldn't be able to be there. In my panic, I didn't think about going to Davenport, but it'd be better for me to be gone. Dahlia didn't prize my opinion. By the time I saw her again, the "returning home" crisis will have all blown over.

"I don't think we're talking about his big toe," I kidded, feeling better already.

She giggled. "Honey, at his age? But it's giving everyone around here something to talk about."

"What do you think? Was he having an affair while his wife was sick?"

"No, Darlin', I can't believe he was. I've known the mayor and Corabelle forever. Her mother and mine were good friends. Both members." She meant members of the Frytown Women's Club. "I'm here to tell you, the mayor worshiped her. This here woman's brain is out of kilter."

"Mr. Atkins says she's out for money."

"You've talked to Paul and Maude?"

"They didn't come for their order today. I wanted to make sure they were all right."

"He said that this woman's out for money?" She paused a half-second. "Why else? An old man might have a roving eye for a younger woman, but what young woman would want an old man? Nothing to be gained other than washing his socks and fixing his meals."

She gave a squeal. "Just a minute, Hon." The phone banged as if dropped. Something clunked open. There was another squeal, this time of delight. She came back on, "I had a batch in the oven. Garth mentioned he'd never had a Ginger Snap. Can you believe that?"

Garth Davis, the rookie cop at the police station. Never having eaten a Ginger Snap cookie was as good as being a virgin to Donna.

"I love Gingersnaps," I said, which when said declared my state of virginity, addiction, and need for recovery when it came to men.

"Then I'll drop you off a batch."

"Thanks, but I need to go out of town." Donna's returning my call was the perfect opportunity. "Can you think of someone who might handle the store for me? Just for a day? I can't pay much."

"I'd do it if it was my day off."

"I know you would."

"Where're you going?"

"Just business."

She thought for a few moments. I knew she was asking herself what type of business I might have outside of Frytown.

"The only person I know who always needs a job is Percy."

Percy Hastings was one of my regular customers, so I wasn't sure he would be a good choice.

"Now, Hon, I know what you're thinkin'. You're worrying Percy'll drink up your inventory. I won't try and convince you he doesn't have a problem. But he's as honest as the day he was born. Just set him a limit. Say, not more than a six-pack. If he agrees, then he ain't gonna open one bottle more until he's off the clock."

Good, grief. A six-pack?

Yet, a six-pack hit Percy no more than caffeine from a cold Pepsi buzzed me.

"And you might offer him...a... well...offer him a bonus. If you know what I mean."

A bonus? Not a bad idea.

Again she asked. "Where're you off to, Hon?"

She'd be asking until she pried it out of me, so I told her.

"Davenport. I might stay overnight. A mini-vacation."

"You deserve it. I didn't know you had friends in Davenport."

"I don't. As I said, this is a business trip. Discount. I need to follow up on some of my suppliers."

"Ah, huh."

Did she believe me?

"Hey, Hon, stay at the Radisson down by the river. It's only a walk from there to the casino. It's got the best all-you-can-eat buffet in the city. They also have the best slots. You can win off them."

"I just might do that. But, I don't gamble much."

"Me, neither, Hon. Not more than I can afford to lose. But I like playin'."

We gossiped further about the mayor's case. Donna said she knew what the mayor was going to say in his news conference. The same as she would. The woman had a screw loose. When I mentioned Bowen's announcement that Jessica Feldman would be on his show, she said, "Bowen's just piddlin' around for a story when there ain't none. Makin' himself look like somebody. That woman hasn't any marriage certificate. If she does, it's a fake. And if I'm wrong, well, I'll give up baking cookies for the rest of the year."

Her saying so confirmed my own thoughts. A fake. Today it was so easy to manufacture something to destroy someone else's life.

"You have my word on it," she confirmed. "Mayor Otis is being defrauded. She's lookin' for fifteen minutes of fame."

Frytown's not a spot on the celebrity map. But I didn't argue. Money or celebrity, Jessica Feldman wanted something.

After I had hung up with Donna, I called out to The Gas for Less by Highway 218. Percy answered the phone.

"Hey, Lillian. If you need to talk to Jasper, he ain't here. His father-in-law's ticker went bust. He took Willa to Cedar Rapids to catch a plane to Florida."

"Sorry to hear the news. Give Jasper and Willa my condolences."

"Sure will."

"Actually, I wasn't calling for Jasper. I need a favor. But if you're covering for him..."

"Only tonight. Need somethin' fixed? That ol' car of yours giving you trouble? I can take a look-see tomorrow."

He was referring to my '98 Mustang convertible. Purchased at a police auction, it came with dents, three bullet holes, and my duck-tape handy work repairing the plastic back window. A real bargain, when it ran.

"The car hasn't given me any problems, lately." I would have knocked on wood, but there was none nearby. The faux wood of my desk didn't count. "If Jasper doesn't need you tomorrow, would you consider watching the store for me?"

"Me?" The offer threw him. "I don't know, Lillian. What if somethin' happened?"

"Nothing happens when you're working at the station, does it?" At least, I'd never heard of any problem. "It's just for the day. I have to go out of town." I added, "I'll pay."

"You don't need to do that. Hell, I'll do it for nothing if you need me."

More than once, I'd had to shove money into his hand for helping out with the car. Donna and Percy. They were two good friends I'd made since moving to Frytown.

"When times get hard, Percy, I'll take you up on that offer. But right now, I can afford it. But if Jasper needs you..."

"He won't."

"All right. How about I meet you at the store right before opening time? Say nine-thirty? It won't take long to show you how things work." As I said, he was a regular, so he knew about most of the stock. I just had to show him how to handle the cash and where to find all the pricing.

After ending the call with Percy, I reconsidered the ridiculousness of my going all the way from Frytown to Davenport to confront Kenny. If I could tell the video was a fake, the police definitely could. Only, there it was again, if I didn't go, and he grew cocky, his ruse could dismantle my privacy. No one knew I had a past. Not even Charles.

Charles Kaefring, Chief of the Frytown Police Department. I worked for the FPD. It was my first job after moving to Frytown. I answered the phones part-time in the mornings. Then I clerked for Discount in the afternoons. That is until I discovered and called in the fire. Became an eyewitness to arson. And Charles thought of our relationship as a conflict of interest. He laid me off.

Several years older than me, he's a Liam Neeson type. Sturdy, manly, and honest, his sexiness came more from what he did than what he said. Although, don't get me wrong. Charles was full of sexual energy.

I'd never met someone like him. Or maybe I should put it in a different way. No one like him ever showed an interest in me.

Turns out, he was married. I've sunk low in my past, but I've never, knowingly, had relations with a married man.

Yet, if I went to him with Kenny's blackmail threat, he'd offer to help. He could turn the table on Kenny and have him arrested.

But as I said, a taint of gossip, valid or not, strongholds a person's reputation worse than a hangover applies a vise-like grip on your head after a night of tequila shots.

Kenny was my problem.

CHAPTER SEVEN   IMAGINE YOU'RE IMPLICATED
OCTOBER 30TH, THURSDAY

"You're here early."

Percy gave a hardy wave. His truck wasn't in Discount's parking lot when I arrived, so I didn't expect to find him waiting for me on the steps.

He stood over six feet with paws for hands, so large they'd hold three of mine. Newly showered, his ruddy complexion glowed from a clean, close shave, and he'd neatly combed his hair. He'd spruced up. Wearing a freshly ironed plaid, cotton shirt, and jeans, he'd shoved his feet into what looked like new boots.

He struggled to a stand, legs like tree trunks. Trying to find a comfortable position for his girth, his muscular arms first crossed, hugging his chest, then uncrossed, and swung back in an at-ease position, before coming to hang resolutely at his side.

"I didn't expect you so early," I smiled. Working in the store was out of his element. He was most comfortable with his head under a car's hood.

"I had Petey drop me off on his way to work."

As far as I knew, and what I'd gathered from Donna, Percy never married and still lived alone. He'd taken care of his mother until she passed. I pictured him by himself, standing at the kitchen sink, forking some of his mother's canned peaches out of a jar, smacking at the syrup.

Petey was his teenage nephew who sometimes worked alongside him out at the gas station.

"Letting him have wheels for the day?" I teased. "He'll be out cruising for girls."

Percy laughed, moving over so I could pass him on the steps. "I told him I knew how much gas was in the tank," he said, "and I expected that much when he came to get me later."

Generally, if you saw Percy in town doing errands, Pete wasn't far behind. "Like two P's in a pod," folks said when seeing them.

He wasn't overly talkative, but his nervousness was making him a Chatty-Cathy. "Heck, I figured since I was going to be here most of the day, he might as well use it. He got his license last month."

"How's he doing?" I put the key in the lock.

"The boy's a born mechanic."

Percy moved into the store behind me. I caught a whiff of a remembered scent, Bay Rum. Or just rum?

Quit it, I chided myself.

He smiled big and proud. "Pete's a good boy. Gets in trouble a bit, but what boy his age doesn't? I can tell you, I was a handful for my mom."

I went over to the front window and changed the CLOSED sign to OPEN. Percy would be okay. Nothing bad would happen. Donna was right. He was honest. If I couldn't trust him, then who could I trust?

When I turned around, I found he'd gone back and was standing on the other side of the threshold. "Percy, it's going to be fine."

"I've never taken care of a store before."

"It has to be a lot easier than getting my old car up and running. If it wasn't, I'd never need you."

He laughed at that. He came in, and I put the key into his callused palm. "Leave the key on the counter after you close tonight or drop it by when I open tomorrow morning. I have a duplicate."

"Tomorrow morning? You're not coming back today?"

"You can close early if you want. Say five-thirty? You don't have to count money or refill inventory. I'll do all of that when I get back. Just turn the sign and lock the door behind you. That easy."

"That easy," he repeated.

His eyes worried to the racks of potato chips, salted peanuts, trail mix, bagged candy, and other munchies. Then they flirted to the cooler offering beers, canned iced teas, energy drinks, cokes, and a few bottles of champagne for those looking to celebrate.

"Come on," I coaxed him forward. "I'll give you the five-minute tour." He still seemed a bit apprehensive, but he followed me back to where shelves offered names like Jack Daniels, Grey Goose, Dewar's, and Cutty Stark. I showed him where I kept the price list for the bottles not clearly price marked. Where he could find special customer orders stored under the counter. How to work the cash register, and how to keep an inventory of those snack items sold. "But, don't worry. If you miss writing down a chip sale or something, it's no bother. I'll catch it when I do inventory. And if you get hungry, go ahead and eat something. Snacks come with the job."

"They do?" He smiled big. "I'll have to tell Jasper. He always makes me pay for chips."

I stood, looking around. Anything else I needed to show him? The store was small and relatively straightforward. The front held the less expensive and customer-friendly items. The back shelved expensive liquors. Snitching a pack of beer or a bottle of André bubbly wouldn't dent my cash flow. Copping a couple of fifths of Wild Turkey or Single Malt Whiskeys would hurt.

I went over to the doorway of a small office behind the counter. "I can't think of any reason you'd need to know what's in here. The shelves are pretty well stocked. This is where I keep extra merchandise. There's also a radio if it's not busy and you want some company."

I glanced back over my shoulder and saw Percy had his eyes trained on the bottles.

"If you get thirsty," I started.

He quickly held up a hand, palm out, stopping me from going any further. "You don't have to worry, Lillian. You know I don't drink when I'm workin'." His hand may have been callused, but it was scrubbed as clean as anyone could get it, having worked around grease and oil most of his life.

"I'm not worried a bit." Okay, I lied a little bit. Clarence told me he never closed the store. "Open seven days a week," he'd stated. I'd only owned Discount for less than two months, and here I was, taking off an entire day.

Worried? Definitely anxious. All night long, my head conjured possible "out of business" scenarios: Percy getting drunk. Having some of his buddies stop by wanting discounts. I could lose my license.

Discounts? What if he gave stuff away.? I couldn't afford that.

I hiccuped.

"You okay?"

"Yeah. Fine." I tried holding my breath and counted to twenty.

He'd dressed neatly and came early. How could I change my mind? Doing so would only confirm to him I didn't trust him. Besides, nothing wrong would happen.

"What I meant was that if you get thirsty, you can have a coke or something. Or a beer. No charge." The best way to hold back trouble is not to have misplaced expectations. "And when you leave tonight, take this home." I pulled a bottle of Jack Daniels off the shelf and placed it on an envelope I'd readied before coming. "A thank you gift." I emphasized, "But only after you close and go home, okay? No drinking and driving."

An owner or employee of a bar or liquor store can't legally consume alcohol until after closing for business. Yet, law or not, I'd be a fool to think Percy was going to get through an entire Thursday-- a fairly light selling day—sitting behind a counter within inches of opening a bottle he couldn't afford and rarely got to partake in. The temptation would be too great.

"Heck, Lillian. You don't need to do that."

But he wasn't looking at me when he said it.

CHAPTER EIGHT

The weather was changing. One day it was nice and warm, the next day rainy. Temperatures had slid from the summer hundreds to fall's sixties. Last night was cold enough to put a shine of frost on the pumpkins setting out on front porches wickedly grinning, waiting for Friday night's trick-n-treaters. In yards, tombstones tilted and warned in large scrawled lettering, ENTER AT YOUR OWN RISK.

As I drove out to Highway 218, taking it to Interstate 80, I marveled at the changing nature. Trees wore their autumn dress of rust, mustard yellow, and striking gold. Cornfields, green in the spring, now harvested, offered fields of dirtied, yellowed, dead stubble.

The drive was relaxing. My hiccups quieted. Everything was going to be all right.

I could have followed I-80 straight to Davenport's city center, but instead, seeing the exit for I-74, I pulled from the fast lane and exited at East Locust Street.

Nostalgia. There was the Rexall Drugs store where at eighteen, my first time away from home, I acquired my first paying job. Stovall's Foods, a block further, was where I clerked after I lost my job at the drug store. McDonald's hadn't changed, teenagers continued to flip burgers. Ronald McDonald offered a big-clown-smile to kiddies, enticing them to come on in, get a Happy Meal. At the Kum and Go, a convenience store for those not wanting to tackle a full grocery, I spotted a man bending over a trashcan searching for recycling.

My first thought was that it was Crazy Ben or a man I named Crazy Ben. He was walking the same route with his shopping cart full of ripped, black trash bags and dirty, smaller white grocery bags, all holding found treasures.

You'd think I'd feel sorry for him. Especially since my life had changed so vastly. I was sober. Getting ahead in life.

Still, I'd once admired how he always seemed to know where he was going. Sure-footed, he traveled the same route, day after day, safe in his routine. Sure of his path. While my path when living in Davenport had taken me on a hamster wheel, running to beat hell, around and around and around, only to end up in the same place.

A toss of life's dice? If I wouldn't have quit drinking, eventually I wouldn't have been able to hold a good job. I might have been pushing around a cart, hoping to find enough recycle to buy a drink to warm my blood, or finding leftover food so I wouldn't have to spend any money on nutritional sustenance.

I slowed. Hold it. Where was his cart? The rusty-wired cart with the squeaky wheels? It was never more than a few feet away in case someone came by, saw the wealth of his booty, and tried to make it his own. Had he been robbed?

I pulled over. I should give him a little money.

I parked. Got out of the car. Ben straightened from the trash, his hands full of empty cans. He must have felt me watching him. He glanced my way.

It wasn't Ben. "What happened to Ben?" I yelled.

He quickly stuffed cans into sacks.

I hurried over. "This is Ben's route."

He pulled out pepper spray. Aimed the receptacle at me. "Get away."

"I'm sorry. I didn't mean to scare you. It's just that my friend Ben has a cart like yours. He walks this route."

He scanned his wares. "Lady, are you nuts? There're dozens of carts like this. Nothing special about me. And I don't know no Ben."

"Well, I'm not really sure what his name was. It's what I called him."

He took the handle of the cart and started to push away. "Get help, lady. You're nuts."

Okay, it wasn't my Crazy Ben, but it was a Ben nevertheless. I pulled a twenty out of my billfold, holding it out for him.

"Get away." He aimed the pepper spray again.

"Here." I held out the bill.

"Go away," he yelled.

"No, you don't understand. This is a gift."

"Get away from me. I'm not doing no harm."

"Of course, you aren't." Poor soul. "Take this. Get a warm meal."

"I don't need your money."

Then he snorted a lungful of air, leaned back, and aimed a huge, slog of spit. It splattered at my feet. He inhaled another mouthful.

I raced back to the car.

What was I doing back here? Why had I come?

After I had pulled away from the curb, I recalled another time, with the original Ben, when one of his sacks dropped off his cart and I fetched to give it back to him. I had to chase him more than a block. When he became winded and I'd caught up, he told me the sack of crushed pop cans weren't his. I told him, I'd seen the sack fall. I showed him how it contained what his other bags carried.

"Ain't mine, I tell you."

Was he so different than me? He was denying his present, while I spent most of my life attempting to deny my past. Maybe we are all Crazy Ben's. Or are they saner? They walk the same routes day after day, hoping for enough to get them by. The rest of us run amuck looking to grab as much as we can before there is nothing left.

I continued down East Locust, conflicted emotions nagging at me. So long ago, Bill Cunningham and I ran away to Davenport days after I turned eighteen. He was set to become a rock star. I was happy being anywhere besides New Liberty, living life as a member of the Dove family. Two weeks after we arrived, he took off in his car without so much as a goodbye. Since we'd been living in his car, I was suddenly homeless. I was without a job other than panhandling, and trying to convince myself I'd rather die than give Dahlia the satisfaction she'd been right.

I'd felt humiliated. Shamed. Wronged. Demeaned. Lesser than any of the other human beings passing me up, avoiding eye contact, and stating, "No spare change," before I asked.

Now, here I was, five years later, moving past people different but same, places familiar but no longer patronized. I was drawn not unlike a moth longs for the warmth and the brilliance of light. I thought I was different, changed, but was I? There were a lot of Crazy Bens. There were a lot of people like me, who thought they could kick their addictions. Walk down streets without hanging their heads. Have others acknowledge their existence.

I wasn't different. The Lillian, who lived in Davenport, was also the Lillian who lived in Frytown. Dissimilar cities, but the same person. Just not drinking. Today.

There had to be something else. I had to believe there was more.

Had it been all bad? No. There had been happy days. I learned how to survive. No one offered me a spare twenty. I was lucky to be offered fifty cents. When Cressie died and I hit bottom, I knew I didn't want to continue walking the same route over and over again, hoping the treasure would get better.

I may have misplaced expectations, but now, at least, I have expectations that aren't pipedreams but are possible achievable realities.

Yet a moth drawn to light isn't watching out for a potential spider web in its path? Spider? Kenny?

I saw the building where I'd spent evenings and most weekends, the Candlelight Bar and Grill. The martini glass emptied and filled. A neon blinking arrow pointed toward the door as if excited to see me. *Here, Lillian. Inside.*

Inside, I knew I'd find a small grill cooking up a burger to go with a lunchtime beer. The front windows showed darker, yet I could clearly see in my mind the red padded bar, worn stools, and a half-dozen tables. When I inhaled, I breathed in the heavy perfume and stench of cigarettes. The bartender would either be at the grill flipping hamburger patties or wiping glasses with a much-used rag. The bartender's name was Bud. *Give me another, Bud.* We'd laugh every time someone ordered a beer. Every time. Every day. *Give me another.*

Did I miss it? Hell, yeah.

It's hard *not* to miss insanity. Being well-balanced doesn't produce the same endorphins.

I put the Mustang into gear and drove away. I traveled to High Street where I once rented a closet of a room in a white, clapboard house. The place appeared smaller. And it had a new coat of paint, a sunny yellow. Flower baskets holding ferns hung above the porch.

Nothing stays the same. That thought was something I could rely on.

I square-cornered back around to East Locust and headed south to Iowa Street, making my way toward the Mississippi River. I drove under the railroad bridge to the street's end, Bechtel Park, before circling around to East River Drive paralleling the waterfront. Before leaving Frytown, I'd taken Donna's advice and made reservations at the Radisson.

A young twenty-something came up to the car as soon as I drove into the hotel's entrance. He was wearing a Radisson white shirt and customary grey pants. He immediately gave my car a worried appraisal. I rolled down the window.

"You can save money by self-parking over there." He pointed.

"No thanks." I stepped out, handing him the keys. "Take it easy on her. You lose a bolt, and she'll fall apart."

He gave me a wide-eyed stare. I pocketed the valet ticket in my jacket, even though he wouldn't be parking the car more than a hundred steps from the self-park area. But I was on a mini-vacation. Treating myself. Reaching into the car, I grabbed my purse and the backpack with my PJs, toothbrush, and the new book I was reading, *Dying for a Daiquiri.*

A hot bath, king-size bed, and a nap.

Before or after Kenny?

With time still ahead and no plans, I couldn't decide. Maybe before and after.

I moved into and through the circular doors allowing visitors to come and leave without heat loss or bringing in cold air. The lobby was a typical four-star hotel with couches and chairs staged to offer conversational niches. Glass tables and contemporary lamps added to the sleek, modern decor. There was a spotting of guests sitting in these prearranged, intimate nooks. A few looked packed for the road trip home, or maybe for the shuttle to take them to the airport.

What looked to be a grandmother sat with a baby crying on her lap and two other children standing at her knees clamoring for her attention. She was glancing over to the man and woman sitting across from her, the parents, who were either using her as a diversion to reap the last few minutes of freedom before being imprisoned by the three on the plane or trying to benefit still from her babysitting before she left. They kept their heads down, their attention on their cell phones.

Several people dressed for business nursed Styrofoam lidded coffee cups, briefcases at their feet. A woman dressed in sweats and an IU tee shirt sat chewing gum zealously as if doing her twenty-minute jaw exercise. Across from her was a guy wearing jeans and a leather grey sports coat, hair a bit disheveled. He raked me with half-closed eyes, taking in my breasts before lowering to my hips. When he came back up for air, I mouthed, "In Your Dreams."

Others were moving away, or toward the restaurant, or coming from their rooms. They were possibly in Davenport on business or on vacation to see the sights: Vander Veer Botanical Park, the Sky Bridge, play the casino boats moored along the river.

Vander Veer Park? I'd never been a tourist.

I noticed a guy looking slightly out of place from all the rest. He had on black leather pants and a black leather jacket, with a helmet setting on the floor by old, dark boots, dull shined as if recently cleaned of mud. His face was buried in a *Quad-City Times* newspaper, and behind the paper, his shiny bald head, well oiled, caught the light from the lamp next to him.

I thought his paper rattled when I walked by like he'd dropped the corner to check me out. Another admirer? Sobriety must look good on me. I never received this much attention when living in Davenport.

A well-groomed attendant came to attention. "Welcome to the Radisson. Do you have a reservation?"

"Yes. Lillian Dove."

The attendant tapped keys on her computer. She asked, "One night? King bed?"

"That's it."

She returned to clicking. "I can give you a better room for the same price. It's on the sixth-floor with a river view."

I wondered what the catch was. "Same price?"

She smiled. "The same price. We aren't that busy today."

"Great, thanks." She took my credit card and swiped it while I held my breath hoping there was still enough to pay for the room.

"Tomorrow will be busy. Weekends always are." She pulled out a sheet paper for me to sign, stating that anything I ordered or used while staying at the hotel, or pinched, could be billed to my credit card.

"One key or two?"

"Two." It's never good to let anyone know you're traveling alone.

She put two key cards into a small, white envelope, wrote the room number on the inside and handed it over. She glanced back at the computer, then said, "There's a message for you. I'll transfer it to your room."

"It can't be for me. I just landed, and no one knows where I'm staying." I hadn't told Percy. And while the hotel had been Donna's suggestion, I mentioned nothing about making a reservation.

"I'm pretty sure it's for you," the attendant returned. "The message came in about three minutes ago, and the caller asked for Lillian Dove. We don't have any other guests by that name. I'll forward the message to your room."

It wasn't for me. It couldn't be for me. But I didn't want to argue the point.

Opening the door to room 602, the large picture window gave view to the great Mississippi, grey, cold, and unyielding. King size bed with king size pillows. A piece of paper put on a plump bed pillow explaining the washing, or non-washing, of towels, thus eco-friendly. A flat-screen television. And on the nightstand next to the bed, a telephone blinking a red message light.

The day so far was too good to ruin. Not the best day I'd ever had, but so far I'd driven through Davenport, becoming a bit melancholy, but not depressed. I tried to keep my thoughts on my priorities. Get rid of Kenny. Kick back and have a good time.

Yet the blink, blink, blinking light wouldn't stop. What if something did happen at the store? What if the police had been called and Donna told Charles where he might find me. I picked up the phone.

"See you at six. If you don't recognize me, don't worry. You haven't changed one bit."

How did he know where I was staying? *The message came in three minutes ago.* Was he in the lobby when I came in?

I shivered.

I grabbed my backpack, hauling everything out onto the bed to find the piece of paper where I'd scribbled his phone number. A number, like the man, I planned to get rid of as soon as possible. I wanted to let him know his ruse to unnerve me didn't work. I wasn't the quiet, cowering person he once knew.

I dialed the number. His answering machine came on. "Your dime. Leave a message."

"Meet *me* at the River Town Brewery. Six-thirty. If you don't show up, I'll figure you don't have shit to show me and I've wasted my time coming to prove you don't." I hung up.

Good. Now I felt better. Somehow I needed to grasp the concept that everything wasn't about me. A blinking light didn't mean something bad happened at Discount. And if it had, was there anything I could do from here?

Enough. I yawned. Nappy time.

After taking a shower and slipping into my PJs—I know, it was barely after two o'clock in the afternoon, but when on vacation, why not live a little?--I gave a call to Discount to double-check everything was going okay. Percy answered on the fourth ring. He apologized, saying the store was pretty busy, being Halloween and all.

"Busy?"

"Don't worry, Lillian. It's not so busy I can't handle it. If they're in that much of a hurry, they can go to the Hy-Vee and spend a dollar more."

Swell. Send them off to the competition. Why not just draw them a map to Walmart? Still, it may be a little busier than I'd expected, but the real rush wouldn't come until Friday night when people would hurry out to the Dollar Store to get a costume and stop at Discount for their party liquor.

I made a mental note to call for a morning wake-up call, no later than six.

After thanking Percy again for covering for me, and adding I knew he'd be able to handle whatever came up, I felt more in control. I turned on the TV. Channel surfed. I stopped seeing Mayor Otis Johns sitting behind his desk in the City Council office.

His family stood around him. "I repeat," the mayor was stating. "I do not know nor have known Jessica Feldman. And while Bobby Bowen's offer to meet her on his show is inviting, I think I will watch the entertainment for ratings from my recliner."

The newscaster came on telling those just tuned in that the mayor of Frytown offered the statement at ten this morning. Since it was a Davenport newscast, the Bowen show was not mentioned or advertised.

I switched the set off. It looked to me as if the mayor wasn't going to back away from frivolous intimidation. A bit stout, never without suspenders, he wasn't exactly the playboy type.

I pulled the mystery novel out of my backpack and curled up on the bed. I read halfway to the second page before the words began to blur together. When I woke up, I found the clock radio showed past four. I'd slept a solid two hours. Taking a glance out the window, the day was quickly coming to a close.

I grabbed the ice bucket and my card key and went in search of vending machines. I popped two bucks into the machine and hit the Pepsi button. This day was only getting better. Pepsi is my coke of choice, and another addiction I'll need to face. Back in the room, I glanced at the telephone. No blinking light. Did that mean Kenny caught the message and was going to meet me at the brewery? Or did he still expect me to meet him at the casino?

I filled a glass with cubes and Pepsi and went into the bathroom to get dressed. But first, I filled up the bathtub for a good long soak. I had time. No need to rush.

CHAPTER NINE

T hursday night is the most popular to go out for dinner or drinks after work. You'd think it would be Friday night. But it seems people start planning for the weekend starting on Wednesday, hump day, and become so anxious for Friday, they can't wait and hit the bars and restaurants heavy on Thursday. In fact, Bud at the Candlelight once told me that he did double the business on Thursday night than he did on Friday or Saturday. He said there was no rhyme or reasoning for it.

My theory is that people have become addicted to their time off from work. They start craving Friday night starting on Monday morning. Those who are really in their cups probably begin obsessing on Sunday evening. The hankering for sleeping in, following no one's rules but their own, nag them, clenches their gut. Every time someone mentions the words Friday, Saturday or Sunday, like Pavlov's dog, they begin to salivate.

My theory held true when I walked into the brewery and the restaurant's acoustics buzzed yammering voices. I strolled around and canvased the place. It was almost seven. I'd purposefully come late planning to knock Kenny further off-guard.

I circled twice, the second time thinking maybe I didn't recognize him. It had been a while. When I was fairly certain he wasn't there, I asked for a small table where I could watch the doorway. Maybe he didn't check his phone messages and went ahead to the casino. If so, he'd be late.

I told the waitress I might be expecting one more person. I took off my jacket, placing it on the back of the chair, tossed my purse under the table, and took the offered menu. I was starving. By the time she came back with my glass of water, I was ready to order a Smoked-Out Bacon Cheeseburger.

It was after the waitress left to put in my order that I saw him. He stood in the entry wearing a light-colored tee shirt under a blue, flannel jacket. His hair, still a little long, fell over his forehead giving him an artistic, playful look. When he spotted me, he held my eyes, his twinkling, and as if there was only the two of us in the room, he walked with his arms out as if to receive a friendly hug.

"Lillian. You look great. Lose some weight?"

I ignored his opened arms. "You don't look so good, Kenny." From across the room, he'd appeared little changed, however, close up, dark circles blighted eyes that were once boyish and charming.

His old-friend smile slowly receded into a grin, then a smirk. He lowered his arms and pulled out a chair, sitting down across from me. I noticed he was wearing Keds, the type worn by kids, blue with white laces neatly tied. He reached over taking my glass of water and sipped from it. "So how'zzz... Frytown?"

I guessed this was the chit-chat phase. "Do you have friends in Frytown?"

"Nah." His eyes shifted around the room. "The place is too small and boring. You know I'm a big city type."

Was I making him uncomfortable? Was he looking for someone? "Let's get right to it, Kenny. What do you want?"

His eyes flicked back to me. He licked his lips and took another sip from my water glass. "Is that any way to talk to a dying man?"

I laughed. "You don't give up, do you?" I reached for my purse and took out my cell phone. I checked the time, seven twenty-three. I showed him the digital. "Two minutes."

"What?" He shirked back. "Aren't you stayin' awhile? Seein' old friends? Relax. We got all night. How about a drink?" He looked around as if searching for the waitress.

"Losing seconds, Kenny."

The waitress interrupted us by bringing my cheeseburger. "Oh, your jacket's fallen." She picked it up and replaced it on the back of my chair.

"Thanks."

Maybe she felt the tension, for she continued to stand, unsure whether to offer Kenny a menu or not? He told her, "I'm not staying for dinner, but I could use a beer."

I checked the phone. Seven twenty-four. "One minute." I pushed the cheeseburger over to him. "Go ahead. There's not enough time to eat."

He stared at me. "You're different. Not as nice as you used to be."

"Whoever said I was nice?" I shot back. "Your friends and I didn't necessarily know one another. I never did drugs. What are you on now? Oxy?"

"Cressie. She said you were nice." He slightly rolled his eyes. "Guess you had her fooled, too."

I flipped the phone's face up again. Seven twenty-five. "Okay. We're done." I stood up.

He reached out and grabbed my arm. "Hold on." He gave the room careful scrutiny. "Sit down, Lillian."

I tried to jerk away.

"It's not a request."

"Let me go." My voice was so loud, the couple next to our table stopped talking and turned toward us.

I seethed, "Let go of me."

He let go, but his voice still held a growl. "I said. Sit down." He pulled something out of an inside pocket of his jacket and placed it on the table in front of me. Small, white, thin, it was a UBS flash drive.

I sat back down, but I let it lay. If I picked it up, then I would be playing his game by his rules.

He tapped the drive with his finger. "This shows you going through Cressie's things and with her lying on the floor next to the bed."

It couldn't. I never went through Cressie's things. His story was as muddled as his mind.

He threatened, "If I don't get a hundred thousand dollars in forty-eight hours, I'm turning this over to the police."

"Where do you think I'm going to get a hundred thousand?"

His eyes flicked again around the room. Then he hunched over the table, picking up my cheeseburger, and took a huge bite. The waitress came with his beer. He grabbed it and washed the cheeseburger down. Burped readily, and grinned. "As I said, I've heard how you're this big business woman. Own a liquor store. Got two houses."

I hated this guy, more than I think I've hated anyone. No, wrong. My tinkers-damn list was fairly extensive. But Kenny was high on it and rising. I took my cell phone and put it back in my purse. "As I said, you're time is up. And your source got it wrong. I inherited the store and house, and the condo belongs to my mother. I'm broke. I'm not even sure my credit card can handle the charge for this cheeseburger. So, I'll let you pick up my tab."

He returned, "Who'd ever give a bitch like you somethin'?"

I leaned toward him, matching his whisper. "Someone who knew I wasn't a bitch and believed in me. Someone better than you." I picked up the flash drive. "Take this to the police, Kenny. I dare you." I plopped it into the glass of water.

"Won't do you any good trying to destroy it. I can make another."

I got up. "Don't contact me again. If you do, you'll be the one behind bars. I kept your phone message." I wished now I hadn't erased it. "Blackmail is a chargeable offense."

I grabbed my jacket and purse and left.

Outside, knees shaking, I hurried to the river overlook a few yards away from the entrance. I hung onto the telescope, rentable for a quarter to watch the tugs and riverboats, and acted like a tourist. But I wasn't watching the water. I was keeping an eye out for Kenny. If he saw me, would he come over to make more trouble? How loaded was he? I never knew him to be dangerous, he always came across as more a flunky, easy prey for bookies and drug dealers, but he'd been combing the restaurant like he was scared he was being followed.

When he came out, his cell phone was stuck to his ear. A tug on the river blasted its horn. Other sounds from people leaving the brewery, late night walkers along the river, kept me from hearing his conversation. All except for, "Tell him to call off the dogs or I'll make sure the Feds are entertained."

I waited, following him until he blended in with the dark ink of nightfall. There was no doubt where he was heading. The casino was close by.

I continued waiting, longer than I probably needed to, but I wanted to make sure he wasn't coming back. I returned to the restaurant. Our table had already been bussed. Two new people were sitting at it.

Catching the waitress at the order desk, punching in an order into the kitchen, I asked her if she found a flash drive. "I think I must have dropped it."

She looked at me kind of funny. I guess it was an odd request. A purse left behind, maybe. Cell phone, more probably. A flash drive? But if Kenny hadn't fingered it out of the glass, I wanted to see what was on it.

"I wondered where you two went." She fooled with the computer while saying, "I didn't see anything, but I had Randy bus the table. We're really busy tonight."

I smiled. "This place is usually busy every night. It's the best restaurant in Davenport."

"Brewery," she reminded me.

"Of course, River Town Beer. My favorite. I don't drink anything but." She handed me a bill.

"He didn't pay?"

She shook her head.

I took out my sadly crippled credit card. "Sorry about that."

She rechecked the amount. "It's only twelve eighty-three."

"I don't have change."

She took the card. Swiped it. I held my breath. It went through. She gave me a pen to sign.

After signing and handing it back, I pulled a five-dollar bill out of my purse. It was either that or count out a handful of change from the bottom of my bag. "Sorry again about my friend. I thought he was going to pay." I offered the bill. "I know you're really busy, but if you could ask Randy, I'd really appreciate it. The drive has a bunch of stuff of my boss's on it, and if I lose it, I'm going to be in hot water."

She looked down at the money, and then back up to me, like, *You have to be kidding?*

I shrugged. "I haven't been to an ATM for a while." As if that would explain the small tip.

"I have an order to pick up." She glanced toward the kitchen. She took the five. After all, money is money. It pays the bills. "I'll check to see if Randy's in the kitchen, but I don't have time to look for him."

"I'd really appreciate it," I said again.

I watched her move back into the kitchen arena. When she came out, she was carrying a tray with food. I figured she'd pocketed my five and blew me off. She didn't even look in my direction. But the guy following her did. He was wearing a dirty white apron and his sweaty face shined with adolescent acne. Randy.

"I found it in the water glass," he said, holding the flash drive out to me. "I doubt it works. Electronics and water don't mix."

"No problem. You've saved my butt. If I lost this, I'd be fired."

He stood, wiping his dishwater wrinkled hands on his apron as if getting ready to receive something. He said, "I almost threw it in the garbage."

"My lucky day." I put the flash drive in my pocket.

"Uh, I had to dig it out of the garbage."

"Oh," as if I just got it. "Didn't the waitress give you the tip?"

His face puzzled, he stretched his neck, looking out over the tables for her.

I turned around and hurried away.

I twirled through the circular doors of the hotel and went over to the reception desk. I asked where I might find the business center for guests. A new shift receptionist pointed down a small hallway. There I found a glass room with two computers, a printer, and a copy/fax machine. Does anyone still fax?

I put the drive into the computer. Nothing booted. I tapped the computer keyboard, waking the screen, brought up Google and typed: flash drive recovery after dropped in water. Several offerings came up. I clicked on the first. The first site mentioned the drive would be damaged or destroyed. So did the second site. Unwilling to give up and not being tech-savvy enough to be sure I posted the search correctly, I continued down the page where there were forums from other clumsy people who had dropped their drives in coffee, toilets, alcohol.

Do not put the wet drive into your computer. Try setting it in front of a fan for a couple of hours to dry out the circuit board. Or better, place it down into a bowl of rice and leave it for a couple of days. Rice will draw out any wetness.

I pulled the drive out of the computer and went up to my room. Not carrying a bag of rice in my backpack, I went into the bathroom for the blow dryer. After standing for what seemed like hours, probably minutes, blow-drying, I went back downstairs and stuck the drive into the computer again. Still nothing. Nada. Zilch. Either I'd zapped whatever was on it by throwing it into the glass of water, or there'd been nothing on it in the first place.

After mulling it over, I decided the second possibility was probably the correct one. Kenny hadn't even bothered to fake a video. He thought I was stupid enough to take him at his word.

His gambling mojo wasn't what it used to be. No, I take that back. He was still throwing craps the hard way.

CHAPTER TEN

The mini-vacation didn't last.

I went to the registration desk to check out. I explained to the new attendant I'd just arrived a few hours earlier but had to leave and asked for my car to be brought around. She appeared distraught. "I hope there was nothing wrong with your stay with us."

"No. I got an emergency call from home and I need to get back."

"Oh. Sorry. I hope it's nothing serious."

"Not serious. Only it can't wait until morning."

Her fingers flew on the keyboard. She glanced up, "You know, I'll have to charge you for the full stay?" She toddled off before I could reply and came back with a sheet of paper she'd pulled from a printer.

"You're charging me for the full night?"

She nodded. "Hotel policy."

Okay, I'd napped on their bed. Used their bathroom. They had a point. But it'd only been a few hours. I challenged, "Then I'll expect to be able to get in my room with this same key if I decide to come back."

"The key cards are changed as soon as..."

"If I am paying for the full time...?" I was in a pretty crappy mood.

"Let me speak with my manager." She hurried off.

"I'll be back by the time my car gets here." I left, heading straight for the elevator. The bell dinged, and the doors opened. I got on. The biker guy who I'd seen in the lobby when I'd first arrived came in behind me. At first, I didn't give him much of a thought, but as the doors closed, I wondered at the coincidence.

Funny how an elevator shrinks when a stranger comes on board, and you're the only other passenger. Especially when that someone looks like a biker skinhead. Only he didn't come across like a skinhead. He was most definitely in the Vin Diesel, Bruce Willis, Dwayne Johnson category.

I pushed the sixth-floor button. He stood, quiet. Was he waiting for me? To do what? I asked, "What floor do you want?"

He glanced at the panel. "Sixth."

The elevator became smaller at the mention of my same number. "Here for a... conference? Or on a vacation?" I babbled, my voice breaking like a teenage boy's.

The light above the elevator doors moved to two.

His shoulders were massive, biceps bulged.

By the third floor, I began to hum nonsensically. A Christmas Carol for god's sake, *Jingle Bells*.

His shirt collar came almost to the base of his chin. The man had no neck.

The light on floor three went out. I prayed someone on the fourth floor was waiting for an elevator. Or parents had just taken a kid back to their room. I swear a kid can't get off an elevator without pushing all the buttons as a joke. Not funny, usually. However, if the doors opened on the fourth floor, I was getting out and hugging the first kid I saw.

The elevator didn't stop on the fourth floor. It continued on to the fifth.

I got the hiccups. It's something that happens when I get nervous. I was getting really, really nervous.

At the fifth floor, he suggested I hold my breath. His voice was low, baritone.

Silly. He could very well be a businessman who liked to work out. He was apparently a man who took care of his body and enjoyed riding a Harley whenever he had some free time.

To show him I was a game-player, I inhaled deeply and puffed out my cheeks.

A red five turned into a red six, and a *ding* announced the sixth-floor. I was still holding my breath and feeling dizzy. I stepped to get off, wobbled and grabbed him to stop from falling.

"Careful." He gently pushed me back.

"I only had one drink." I joked.

That's when I noticed a cobra's head tattooed above his wrist, a snake's body stretching up under his jacket. I made a small animal sound.

Had I wobbled, or had he pushed me? Now, I wasn't certain.

He reached out toward me. I flinched. His hand moved to the panel, he punched the L button. Seeing what must have been a shocked expression on my face, he said, "Forget something?"

I raced out of the elevator and down the hallway. I dipped the key card into the slot, green light, and closed the door securing the security hook.

One thing, the hiccups were gone.

I took off my jacket and tugged off my jeans. I was hot but cooling down fast. The flash drive from the brewery dropped to the floor. I went to throw the useless drive into the wastebasket and then thought better of it. I picked up the novel from off the bed and put the flash drive inside to hold my place.

I changed back into comfortable jeans, gathered my stuff from the bathroom, and shoved everything into my backpack. I grabbed my jacket, unlocked the door and glanced down the corridor. Empty. Relief. I continued to keep an eye out for biker guy as I got back in the elevator.

The Mustang waited in the turnaround. Again, I glanced around the lobby. I took a relieved breath. Maybe he was just a guest who'd wanted to read his paper in the lobby instead of his room, and he just happened to decide to go up at the same time I did, but then saw he'd misplaced his...his...paper?

I didn't bother having another bout with the registration attendant. Instead, I went immediately outside. The businessman in the grey sports coat was leaving. He'd stopped, I guess, to admire my car. Many do. Not that it's unusual to drive a vintage Mustang. It's the bullet holes that gandered interest. Or the back yellowed-plastic window duck-taped into place.

He got into his own black, Toyota Land Cruiser with cartoon figures in the back window: husband, wife, two kids, a dog, and a cat. Middle America.

I flagged the valet. Reaching into the pocket of my jacket, my fingers felt the valet card, and something else. I pulled out a small, flat, baggie. The outside was stamped in red, Pay Dirt. Inside was a white powder.

How did THAT get in my pocket? Kenny? No, I didn't let him get anywhere near me. The guy in the elevator? But I'd bumped into him, not him into me? Didn't I?

Terrorized by what I was holding, I glanced quickly around. Was someone watching? The valet had his eyes on long, tanned, naked legs getting out of the car across from mine. I stuffed the baggie back in my pocket.

I got behind the steering wheel, put the Mustang into gear, and took off.

No nostalgia now as I turned corners, heading for the interstate. I pulled into traffic. The Pay Dirt in my pocket felt more like a scorching hot rock. Had someone mistakenly given it to me? Someone from the restaurant? Or was this a free sample?

I reached in and took the small baggie out. Pay Dirt. Heroin? Coke? With no prior drug knowledge, I didn't have a fathom what Pay Dirt could mean. To end the paranoia, I opened the window and threw it out.

The car behind me honked. Apparently, he thought I was littering.

Merely minutes later, I saw lights flashing. It was an unmarked car with a flashing light on the dash. I pulled across lanes to the far shoulder. Scott County was serious about it's *Keep Iowa Beautiful* campaign. I'd seen a billboard advertising such, but I didn't think the state was bothering to stop motorists, writing fines for littering. Not when they were losing the war on drugs.

I kept my hands on the steering wheel. If you drive a car with bullet holes and dents, the police could get the wrong idea. Best to be on good behavior. Traffic zipped and roared past.

I rolled down the window. "Is there a problem, officer?" I smiled.

He didn't. Tough guy. "I stopped you for exceeding the speed limit. Driver's license and registration, please."

Speeding? Not littering?

Rule one: Be nice. The police put up with a lot of crap. Rule Two: Move slowly. You don't want them thinking you're going for a weapon.

So, in slo-mo, I reached into my purse and retrieved my license out of my wallet.

He took it and shined his flashlight on it.

"Not my best photo," I joked.

His expression remained chiseled stone.

Rule Three: Be courteous and compliant. "I'll get my registration. It's in the glove box."

Again, I moved slowly, opened the glove box, sorted through the empty candy wrappers, chip sacks, used and unused Kleenex, and plastic packages of Dairy Queen ketchup.

I'm faithful at putting the new registration into the glove box as soon as I get it in the mail, but I'm not as faithful in removing the old ones. I handed him the wad. "The newest is in there. You'll find it faster with your flashlight."

"Get out of the car." He ignored what was in my hand.

Evidently, he wasn't willing to do the sorting. "Okay. Here. I'll find it."

"Remove yourself from the car." He said it louder as if I hadn't heard the first time.

"Sir, I'll admit I may have been going sixty-five, seventy. I'm heading home. But I believe I was not excessively speeding."

He ordered again. "I said, get out of the car."

A jolt of uneasiness ran through me, and even though there was still a good deal of traffic, I felt intimidated and vulnerable.

"I want to know why you want me to step out of my car. I believe I have that right." Yet, to demonstrate I was a law-abiding citizen, and not wanting to aggravate him into awarding too high a ticket, I got out.

"Hey!"

He shoved me against the car. "Put your hands on the roof where I can see them." He patted me down.

"Hold on. What are you doing?" I turned around, stunned. "You're searching me for a speeding violation?"

He had a square Clint Eastwood jawline and was dressed like a State Trooper in a chocolate brown shirt with tan epaulets, tan trousers, and black shoes. I wanted his name, thought I'd put in a complaint about police brutality. His shield was pinned to his shirt, state seal prominent, Eagle design, with red enameled ribbons. I was familiar with the badges. His read *Officer*. However, I zeroed in on what was missing, no name tag above the badge. And the badge insignias on the sleeves of his shirt, and the insigniaspinned on his collar identified him as a lieutenant. Something wasn't right. Lieutenants didn't work patrol.

He threatened, "We can do this the easy way, or the hard way. I can arrest you for resisting a police officer."

"Me? Resisting?"

He jerked me over to in front of the car. Planted my hands apart on the hood. Kicked my feet straddle. "Stay here, and don't move."

I watched through the front windshield as he found my backpack and unloaded its contents on the ground next to the car. His flashlight did a quick survey. Then he reached back inside but found out my interior lights didn't work. Not a surprise with the condition of my car.

The spot of light popped back inside. He emptied my purse on the seat. Coins tinkled and clinked. My cell phone tumbled out, and I heard it hit hard on the asphalt.

"Hold on. You're ruining my stuff."

The flashlight burned my eyes. "Don't move. Not one inch." He picked up the phone, played as if to open the screen, but it was password protected.

Anger mounted, pushing away any fear. "You're a lieutenant." There, now, he knew he wasn't fooling me. "Why are you working patrol? I demand you call for back up."

The flashlight punched me again. "Do you want me to taser you?"

Blinking, spots on spots, it was hard to see clearly. However, what he was pointing at me had to a taser or a gun.

Pepper spray and taser, all on the same day? Geez. Someone would think I was the bad guy.

I had little choice but to stand at the hood, headlights from oncoming traffic continuing to blind-sight me, as well as his flashlight punching. I wasn't going to move an inch. I was at the station when they tasered Garth before giving him his gun. It's a requirement for being issued one so the officer has an awareness of the potential injury. Garth fell to the ground at impact and twitched for at least a couple of seconds. And his was a light dose.

Apparently thinking the taser threat was enough to keep me submissive, he crawled into the car, flashlight bobbing, and searched the front and the back. Still finding nothing, or not what he was looking for, he came out from the car, walked around and opened the trunk. He wasn't going to find anything in there. I didn't even carry a spare tire, which Percy warned me would be a huge mistake because the tires on my car were going bald.

He slammed the truck lid closed. Walked to where I stood. The spots in my eyes gave him a distorted image. Or maybe it was his expression of irritation. "Where is it?"

"What?"

"Don't play stupid with me. I know you're holding."

Holding? Drug language. He was talking about the baggie of Pay Dirt. How did he know about it? Who sent him? Kenny?

It took every nerve in me to stand still, erect and quiet, as I waited for him to make the next move. When he didn't, I dared to suppose not having what he was looking for actually gave me the upper hand. "We'll call this situation mistaken identity. I can make this easy for *you*. Let me go, and I won't see your commander or a lawyer about an illegal search. Or, if you prefer the hard way, give me a ticket or arrest me and I'll see you in court."

I eased around him, expecting him to stop me. As I passed, I could feel the heat coming off his body. Anger? Arrogance? I was not only threatening his command but also his male ego. Yet, if I showed any fear that he was right and I was wrong, the situation could quickly flip. He could arrest me.

I walked to where my things lay scattered on the ground. Picking them up, I threw the mess into the car. I held out my hand. "I'd like my cell phone back."

His eyes squinted down. His hands moved to his duty belt. "Make my day."

Okay, he didn't say that.

He came toward me. I flinched. However, he walked around me and went back to his car, got in, and drove off.

"If you're a friend of Kenny Litky's," I shouted, "tell him it didn't work. Tell him he can check into my bank accounts. They're empty."

How had Kenny got a lieutenant in the State Patrol to do his bidding? More blackmail?

I got in the car. Pulled into traffic. I moaned a lungful of panic. What the hell had happened?

The thought immediately gave me a wary suspicion my trip to Davenport might not be the end but the beginning of more trouble to come.

I kept vigilant as I drove back to Frytown. I moved lanes, several times, with the sole purpose of catching another car shadowing my movement.

Nothing.

Yet, it wasn't until I took the I-74 exit that a sense of total relief came over me.

Seeing the Gas for Less sign at the 218 Exit offered reassurance. I promised, no matter what Kenny conned, I was never stepping foot in Davenport again.

CHAPTER ELEVEN

A patrol car pulled out of the chain-link gates of the Frytown Police Department as I drove by, forcing me to hit the brakes. Red and blue lights whirled. I recognized the car as Officer Dick Cooney's car, Number 26. I glanced at the time. Nine o'clock. Dick worked third shift, so he shouldn't have been on duty for another hour.

I followed him. Each block we drove ramped my nerves. I ignored the turn I'd normally take to home. Something was wrong. I could sense it.

Reaching the corner of Lakeview Road, I saw flashing emergency lights in front of Discount.

I pulled behind Cooney's car and got out. "Hey, Cooney. What's going on?"

He jerked around, surprised to find someone running up to him. "Lillian, is that you?"

An ambulance was parked in the lot, back doors open. Percy? I bolted past Cooney, ignored others who saw me coming and who called out my name. I ran up the steps, pushing past Officer Garth Davis, who held out his hand as if to stop me. The harsh sting of barley and malt hit me. The store reeked.

"Where's Percy? What's happened?"

Dumbfounded, I saw snacks on the floor, crunched and flattened. I could see the shelves near empty. "Oh, my God." In a daze, I moved toward the back. "Who did this?"

Sergeant Wheeler poked his head out of the small office behind the counter. "Take it easy Lillian. Everything's okay."

Not even close to my assessment. "Where's Percy?"

He raised an eyebrow and tipped his head. I moved through the counter access, slipping around Sergeant Wheeler. Percy was sitting on the stool I kept behind the counter. With him was Larry Madden, one of Frytown's four paramedics.

Percy's shirt was off, his body bandaged, and where the skin was exposed, his body showed raw, red scrapes. His left arm was positioned in a sling. Larry was hooking up an IV bag.

"Percy, are you okay?" What I was seeing didn't compute.

Percy immediately glanced away.

"Okay, Percy. Let's get you to the hospital." Larry went to help him off the stool.

"Hell, I'm all right," Percy snapped, repelling assistance. "I don't need no hospital." He peeked at me beneath lowered eyes. "I sure am sorry about all this."

Sorry? What did that mean? Why was he sorry? I knew he hadn't done this. "Are you okay?"

He nodded.

Larry didn't agree. "He may have a fractured his arm, along with other contusions and abrasions. He's lucky he didn't break his fool head." He gave his attention back to Percy. "I'm taking you in for x-rays."

"Ah, hell." But this time, he let Larry help him off the stool.

As he came over to where I stood, the scrapes on his shoulders, chest, and protrusive stomach appeared far more severe than either Larry or Percy were making it sound. The bloody skin likened to patches of raw meat.

"I'll need you to tell me what's missing." Sergeant Wheeler was at my side. Corbin Wheeler still retained his summer tan. His thick grey eyebrows matched his bush of a mustache, and his manner was gentle but commanding.

My concern had changed from the disaster I'd found in the store, to the possibility Percy was badly hurt. I told Wheeler, "It can wait. I need to go to the hospital with Percy."

"Percy's going to be all right. He's been roughed up, but Larry doesn't think his injuries are critical."

Critical? A meat grinder would have done less damage to a pot roast.

Yet, I stayed, unsure what I would be able to do for Percy if I did go to the hospital. "I don't understand." I peered out from the office, surveying the ruin, and the enormity of what had taken place. It was beyond any invented, probable worse-case-scenario. And none of it added up. It was as if my brain couldn't take it all in. As if somehow my eyes were being tricked. As if, at any moment I expected someone to leap out shouting, *Gotcha.*

Wheeler explained. "Percy said the perpetrator came into the store when he was closing. He said he hadn't seen the guy before, and he was pretty sure it wasn't someone from around here. The guy was wearing some sort of mask. Ski mask is how Percy described it. Percy said before he could get around the counter, the guy pulled a baseball bat and started swinging. Caught him off-guard."

My mind stuck on the idea of a ski mask. It wasn't yet Halloween.

I left the office and assessed the damage from this different angle. The refrigerated section looked unharmed, which was the only good in all the wrong. A new refrigerator would have cost a bundle.

Wheeler followed me. "Percy said he got a hold of him and wrestled the guy to the ground. He thought he punched the man out, and with Percy's size and strength, that wouldn't take much. He said he was going back into the office to call the police when the guy came up behind him and knocked him down hard. He struck Percy's shoulder. Larry thinks if it's not broken, it's fractured pretty bad. Percy's lucky. Could have been his head.

"Percy said it happened in a matter of seconds. The guy grabbed a few bottles and headed out. Percy chased him clear to his car, got a good hold again on him through the car window, but the guy threw on his brakes, and Percy said his shoulder gave and he had to let go."

"Why didn't he just let the guy go? Call you guys?"

Wheeler nodded, then shook his head. "By then, Percy wasn't thinking and he was pretty damn mad at being caught off-guard. The car dragged him a good two hundred feet before he was thrown loose."

"Oh my God." I could imagine all of it.

"He can be stubborn as a mule and as brazen as a bear when he thinks he or one of his friends has been done wrong." There was a note of admiration in Wheeler's voice. Percy might be low on ambition, and he drinks too much, but he held respect for the way he'd taken care of his invalid mother and how he would, without a second's thought, pull off his only clean shirt to give it to someone else to dirty.

Wheeler waited for me to take in all Percy had done before going on to give the rest of the story. "Tom Stark across the way said he heard the commotion and checked out his front door. He witnessed the part where Percy was forced to let go. He said a motorcycle came out of nowhere and pulled in front of the car. The driver braked to avoid crashing, and that's when Percy was jerked clear."

"Stark said when he got to Percy and saw him, he was afraid the fool was going to die. He got Percy back inside the store and called us."

"He's lucky he didn't get killed." I might have never forgiven myself if he had. Even so, I felt guilty as hell.

"Percy said you'd gone out of town. He was working for you?"

I nodded. "I wasn't planning to come home until early tomorrow morning. But my plans changed."

He took out a pad of paper and made a note. "He said he'd closed up and was helping himself to a little..." He paused. "He called it a bonus? When the guy came in."

I wondered if the "bonus" would go down in the report. If so, I wasn't just out of business from all the destroyed product, but my license pulled. "Pete was supposed to pick him up."

"Pete Baker?"

I nodded. "Pete dropped him off this morning. Percy said Pete was going to use the truck and then would pick him at closing."

"I haven't seen Pete." He made another note on his pad.

The timing of the bonus and the information on Pete coming to get Percy at closing would go in the case timeline. By the time the investigation was finished, it'd be known whether Percy started his bonus before closing or not.

Officer Garth Davis interrupted coming over to report to Wheeler. "I went house to house but most everyone was glued to their sets with the mayor's trouble. Stark was the only one who heard the commotion and says the car was a beat-up old Honda. Dark in color. He didn't catch the plates. He didn't get a good look at the biker, either."

Wheeler thought out loud. "Lonnie Muller two blocks over has friends who own bikes."

"Muller? Any relation to Rod Muller?" Garth asked.

"His older brother."

Garth nodded. "I'll check it out. See if any of his friends were in the area." He paused. "But I doubt whoever did this was anyone from around here. And not a friend of Muller's. They would have stopped seeing Percy."

"Agreed. But ask around anyway. Maybe they didn't see Percy."

Garth looked unconvinced. "Hard to miss ol'Percy." He said, "If a bunch of them had been drinking over at Muller's, maybe whoever pulled in front of the car, stopping it, took off worried they were in the wrong."

"Possibly." Wheeler directed, "I want the entire street blocked off. I'll have the techs check for tire threads. And if Percy got a right hook on the guy, maybe we'll find some blood other than his." Wheeler cautioned Garth, "No one, and I mean no one, is allowed in the store other than those who need to be."

Gath took off. Wheeler turned to me. "I'll need you to stick around for awhile, Lillian."

Wheeler went back to the investigation, and I went over and sat on a bumper on one of the parked patrol cars where I would be out of the way but still within hearing distance. Officers passed, offering their commiserations. When Officer Miner strolled over, I started to get up thinking Wheeler must have asked him to come for me, but he waved me back down.

"Stay where you are, Lillian. You're not wanted, yet. Wheeler says he already has too many people mixing their DNA with the crime scene. He's waiting for the Chief to get here before doing much more."

Upon mentioning the Chief, a black Ford Explorer drove into the parking lot. Chief Charles Kaefring got out.

Wheeler must have been watching for him or someone mentioned the Chief's arrival because Wheeler came out of the store and walked over to the SUV before Charles got out from behind the wheel. Wheeler pulled out his writing pad and went about informing Charles what he'd learned so far. Wheeler then pointed over to where Miner and I were sitting.

The two men headed to the store. They hadn't got inside before a squeal of tires punctured the subdued atmosphere. A yellow Corvette drove into the parking lot, braking hard. Detective of Major Crimes Jacque Leveque got out of the car.

Leveque was respected for his position by the other officers. He was also highly admired by some for his ability to turn female heads. He self-proclaimed there wasn't a woman alive who could resist his...charms? Sexual magnetism?

Okay, he was hot.

Only, I wasn't so charmed. And I'd taken a vow to stay away from men like him.

He tried his magic on me when I first started working for the police, and I told him to get lost. Men had been an addiction for me during my drinking days, and like booze, I was working my recovery. My dating Charles was different. Charles was far above the other men in my life. He was a professional. Respected.

As it turned out, he wasn't so different. He was married.

Leveque swaggered over. He was wearing a tee-shirt with the sleeves torn out and jeans with the waistband riding low on his hips. When he lifted his arms just right, the bottom of the tee-shirt lifted and dark hair trailed from his exposed navel.

Not that I noticed.

"Chief inside?"

Miner nodded. "Just got here."

"Heard Percy got roughed up pretty bad."

"Took a ride on the pavement. He tried to stop the guy from leaving."

"If anyone could, it'd be Percy. Big as a bear and twice as strong." Leveque must have been having dinner when the call came in. He moved a toothpick across his lips with his tongue.

Miner concurred. "Someone on a bike pulled in front of the driver, knocked Percy away. They just took him to the hospital. He's skinned up but nothing broke, I don't think."

"Where were you?"

His question was for me. I'd been listening to the conversation but my attention had been in keeping an eye on the store waiting for Charles to come back out.

I would have ignored the question, but it was asked with such a tone of accusation, I couldn't dismiss it. "Out of town. I just got back."

Leveque might be eye-candy for some, but he was a pain in my backside most of the time.

"Out of town, where?"

"Just out of town."

"That wasn't what I asked."

"How is it relevant?"

He shifted the toothpick to the other side. He glanced to Miner, lifted an eyebrow as if to ask—can you believe this shit—and returned to me with an air of displeasure. "I'll tell you how it's relevant..."

But it's all the further he got. I caught Wheeler signaling to me. As I stepped away, I heard Miner say, "Lillian was in Davenport on business."

"Business?" Leveque scoffed.

Suddenly a hand latched onto my shoulder. "Hold on," he ordered. "I'll need to get a statement from you."

I shrugged him off. "I have nothing to say. To you."

I'd be required to report my whereabouts eventually, but I wasn't going to make it easy for him. His ballooned ego asked to be popped, and I carried a very sharp pin.

Charles wasn't dressed in his usual pressed uniform but in jeans and shirt. Beneath raven black hair, he had clear blue eyes. So blue, so clear, I could almost see myself reflected in them.

"I heard you were out of town when this all happened, Lil. I want to warn you before you go inside, the place is a mess."

"I know. I've already been inside."

"Good. Then you won't be distracted looking for what's missing. Cash. Merchandise."

"Chief?"

He looked to someone behind me.

"Neighborhood canvased?" Leveque stood a breath away from me.

Charles nodded. "Wheeler said Garth questioned the neighbors. Tom Stark's the only witness so far. Or at least he observed Percy dragged down the street. I instructed Garth to take Stark on down to the station to get his statement."

"I'll still need to speak to him."

"Granted, but it's late. I told Garth to try to take down the relevant details and to tell Stark you'd get back with him tomorrow. Besides, from what Garth said, Stark didn't get much."

Leveque looked into the store. "They did an impressive job, didn't they?"

"Only one guy from what Percy's said." Charles added. "Took a baseball bat to the place?"

"And to Percy?" Leveque asked.

"Yeah. But most of his injuries come from being dragged down the street."

Leveque mused, "Seems funny, doesn't it?"

I noticed the toothpick was missing when he moved a bit closer to me. "Don't you think it's pretty strange Percy didn't try to stop the guy from busting up the place?"

"What are you implying?" I asked. "That Percy had something to do with this?"

"Nah, but Percy may have recognized the person. I thought he was a friend of yours. Let him in."

"I don't have friends who would do something like this," I retorted. "Do you?"

"Not me." He turned to the Chief. "It might be good for me to get Stark's statement now. While everything's fresh in his mind. If he saw the make of the car and caught a number or two of the license plate, we could put it out to the State Patrol. Have them watch the highways."

"I think it'd be a waste of time for now. Stark said he thought it was an old car. Honda was his guess. Didn't catch the plate. Percy might be able to give us more. Why don't you go ahead and get his statement before they start pumping painkillers into him? I'll stay here until the investigative team is finished. I'll meet you back at the station."

Leveque gave me a grin. "I could stay here and handle this situation if you wanted to speak to Percy yourself."

"Nah, you go. I'm needed here."

Leveque might play big guy around me, but he controlled his self-importance when it came to Charles. "Got it." He asked Charles, "Percy say if he recognized the guy?"

Charles shook his head. "He told Wheeler the guy was wearing a ski mask."

Again, Leveque said to me, a cockiness in his attitude, "Dating anyone who likes to ski, Lillian?"

No way I was going to let him get to me. "I have a long list of ski bum lovers, Leveque."

"I could have guessed the bum part."

Charles grunted and ordered, "The hospital, Leveque."

"On my way."

He took off and Charles directed me to the store. "Sorry about that, Lil."

"Yeah, I'm sorry for him, too. When are you planning to replace him?"

"He's a good detective," he said.

"Good for whom?" I didn't wait for him to answer. The answer, at least from my viewpoint was redundant. Good for Leveque, of course.

Re-seeing the scatter on the floor, my infuriation for Leveque quickly dissipated.

Tears welled.

"You okay, Lil?"

"No," I said. I started shivering but wasn't cold.

He pulled me close. "Don't worry. You'll get through this."

I shook my head. "No, I won't."

"It probably looks worse than it is."

If someone had told me the store had been hit by a tornado, I wouldn't have doubted them.

I wanted to believe Charles, but the truth was evident. This was bad.

Only his expression of sympathy and tenderness held me. I tried to smile. "How could it be worse?"

He squeezed my arm. "This could have happened when you were here, not Percy. You could have been hurt."

I moved closer, trembling, wanting the warmth he offered.

I could sense him wanting to pull me into his arms, and I wanted to let him.

If we were in another place? At another time?

Officer Miner interrupted, moving us apart. "Chief. Give me a minute?"

While Charles went with Miner, I watched the investigative tech team, Officers Carmine Roth and Tony Fisher, dust for latent prints. Black powder like fairy dust sprinkled the air, shelves, racks, and floor. I checked the front door expecting to see damage from having been broken into, but there was no hint of force.

Had Percy let him in? Was the person who did this someone he knew? Or had someone come before he had a chance to lock up? Surprised him and caught him off-guard?

"I'd like you to check the registry first." Charles came back and moved around me, leading me toward the back of the store.

He stayed in front of the counter while I went behind to where I kept the cash. Clarence didn't have a register, and I hadn't changed the place much from how he'd kept it. Sales weren't multitudinous on a daily basis making accounting cumbersome. In other words, there was no reason to keep the door ajar from the amount of traffic moving in and out. We'd get ten, twenty, thirty customers a day. Some were kids on their way home from school, stopping for cokes, chips or candy. On this side of town, Discount worked, too, as a convenience store. Clarence used to keep a stock of milk and bread and some necessities. That's one change I'd made. Once these items were depleted, I didn't reorder. Just not enough need.

Like him, however, I kept money in a drawer and hand- tallied most sales. If audited, I might have to invest in a better accounting method.

Opening the drawer, I was stunned to find so much cash. Far more than I expected. When I'd telephoned, Percy said the place was busy, but at first glance, it looked more like the weatherman announced a blizzard and everyone wanted to stock up for a freeze.

"I left Percy around two hundred in change There's quite a bit here." I offered, "Do you want me to count it?" I finger-flipped through the twenties. "There's more here than that."

Had Percy run the robber off before the cash drawer was found? Or was the guy on a drugged-drunken high, interested more in the booze than in money?

But that didn't make sense. On a high, looking to get higher, no criminal I ever heard of would do this much damage without aiming to steal cash.

Did Percy refuse to show him where the money was kept? Percy said the guy had hit him. Yet, Percy was the one who threw some punches until the baseball bat was brought out.

Baseball bat? No gun? Why would someone robbing a place, for the money or booze, use a baseball bat as a threat and destroy everything within reach? It'd take too much time. Someone could have come in on him.

Unless he thought I was the one in the store and not Percy. Percy was the surprise.

"Count it later, Lil. Percy must have run him off before he got the cash." Charles glanced around. "Anything else of value taken?"

I shut the cash drawer. "Everything was valuable to me. It's all ruined."

Charles said, "I seem to remember Clarence kept a gun. You still have it?"

I glanced at the shelf where it was kept. I hadn't touched the gun since taking over the store. As far as I knew, Clarence never had need of it. "It's here." I started to bend down to verify it was still in place, but I stopped hearing Charles's next question.

"Are you licensed to use it?"

"I've never used it. It's Clarence's."

"If it's on the premises then it's considered yours. Under the law, you need to register it in your name."

Okay, if I would have thought about the gun, I'd have known I needed to record it. But I hadn't given the weapon a thought since pulling it out to threaten Edgar Pike back last summer. And then, I'd been so nervous handling it, I'd dropped the gun on the floor."

The gun was the last thing on my mind. Keeping the store in the black was my higher priority.

My foot kicked a bottle of Grey Goose, sending it rolling. With the distraction, I changed the subject. "There's an inventory list in the office, but I think it's going to take me some time to figure out what's left. If anything."

"You're insurance should cover a situation like this?"

"Of course. Sure. My insurance will cover everything."

But like the gun, if Clarence had any insurance, it wouldn't apply to me because I hadn't switched any insurance into my name or applied for new.

Charles went on. "Wheeler said there wasn't any computer found in the office. Could it have been taken?"

He came around the counter and we both moved into the room. Computers are eye-candy for addicts. They can be easily carried out a door or through a window. Sold fast. Seeing no cash register, the guy might have grabbed what he could once he had Percy down for the count.

I shook my head. "I keep the computer at the condo."

In the office, bloody gauze spotted the floor around the stool where Percy had been sitting. Again, the thought of something worse happening to Percy stirred my thoughts. What if I was somehow responsible?

He didn't get a good look at the biker. The guy took off as soon as the driver hit his brakes.

Charles placed his arm around my shoulder. I sighed into his embrace, again letting him carry the heaviness that came over me. This was too much. I wouldn't be able to survive all this.

"It'll be okay, Lil. It looks bad now, but once things get cleaned up, you'll find it's not as bad as it looks."

He kept saying it, but he didn't have the total picture. He didn't know about Kenny's threat, yet. He didn't know why I'd gone to Davenport. What would he say if I told him drugs had been planted on me, and I'd been stopped by the State Patrol?

I pulled slightly out of his embrace. Honest. Straight forward. Caring. He offered what I'd felt had been lacking my entire life. Acceptance. Safety. Love.

He said, "Do you have any idea who did this, or why?"

I wanted to tell him everything right then and there. But I didn't. Maybe I had it all wrong. Maybe what happened to the store had nothing to do with Kenny. Maybe I was connecting lines to coincidental dots.

Someone cleared his throat. Investigative Officer Tony Fisher stood in the doorway, appearing somewhat uncomfortable. "Done here, Chief."

"Do your inventory in the morning, Lil," Charles suggested. "Since you were just coming back into town when this occurred, your statement can wait. I'll have Leveque come around tomorrow. If we got even a partial and the guy has a record, we'll find out sooner than later who did this."

Charles waited while I got into my car before getting into his SUV. He followed me all the way home. I parked in the garage and walked around to the front of the building. I waved. Only then did his headlights move across the building.

I went to take out my phone to call the hospital. If Percy was still there, maybe I'd go and make sure he was all right. I knew I wouldn't be able to sleep until I was sure he wasn't badly hurt. Then, I remembered. No phone. I also remembered seeing the patrol officer trying to get past my password. He'd taken my phone.

I went back to the garage. Questions were flying through my mind faster than I could access any answers.

I skipped the hospital and went straight back to the store. I grabbed a trash can, broom, and dust bin. I started closest to the door. A few of the bagged snacks were salvageable but most had been trampled and ruined. Probably from the police coming and going, and techs working their part of the investigation.

I worked from front to back. When I moved behind the counter to sweep the broken glass, my foot again kicked the Grey Goose bottle. This time, I picked it up. Not a crack in it. Broken bottles, smashed glass, and puddles of alcohol, but this Grey Goose survived.

I started to put the bottle back on a shelf but stopped. Vodka is vodka. Grey Goose, Absolut, Smirnoff, they are all the same except for the price. People drink Vodka because it's easy on the pallet and doesn't weep through pores like gin or Jack. My poison of choice had always been Absolut for some of those same reasons. I also liked how saying its name worked my mouth, making my lips move with the syllables, my tongue touching behind my teeth with the hard T at the end.

It was a word of unquestionable exactness for someone who never felt she'd had an authentic, legitimate, resolute moment in her entire life.

My fingers played with the edge of the glued label holding down the cap. I gripped it as if to twist. The papered label gave slightly. "What the hell?" The words floated through my mind as if offering a justified reason for giving up before I figured out how I'd gone wrong.

The telephone in the office rang. I set the bottle on the shelf.

"Lillian? I wasn't sure you'd still be there."

"Percy, are you all right?"

Then as if we were in chorus, "I'm so sorry."

"Damn, if I'd have seen he was carrying a bat," he spat, "I would've been ready for him. I'd have given him back some of what he dealt. But I didn't see it. Honest, Lillian. He clocked me one against the head before I had a chance to say howdy."

"Did you get a good look at him? Was he from around here?"

"Nah, I didn't know him from Adam." He paused. "I called to make sure you were okay. I'll pay for any damages."

Was he feeling responsible because the incident happened on his watch? Or was he lying? Had he known the person?

I told him again that it wasn't his fault, and what he could do for me was to get better. "Get some rest. The police will find out who did this." And then I said, maybe to make him feel better, "the insurance will cover the loss."

I finished cleaning as much as I could and then decided, like Charles suggested, to wait to do the inventory in the morning. I wasn't sure I'd be able to sleep, but the more I threw in the trash, the more depressed I became. The more I thought, the more I became sure that Kenny calling me and my going to Davenport had something to do with what happened. If Kenny was connected, if out of spite he did this, or had someone do it, Percy wouldn't need to take care of anything. I wasn't going to let someone like Kenny Liky destroy my life.

I went to leave, turned the key in the lock. That's when I noticed. The sign was changed to CLOSED.

CHAPTER TWELVE

I t was well after midnight by the time I got back to the condo. As I made my way inside the building and moved down the corridor, an old friend glided next to me. A faithful companion, denial was never far away.

It'd sat in the passenger seat when I moved to Frytown, seducing me. *You don't have any choice. Frank left you with no choice.* She's going to die soon. *It'll be better then.* Cold, dark, beckoning. Whispering its alluring embrace. Ensnaring me in its safe arms.

It matched my steps, listening to my silent plea. *You'll wake up in the morning. It'll all have been a horrible nightmare.*

I pushed my key into the lock.

I heard a clunk.

Bacardi?

I'd left him enough food and water, but that wouldn't stop him from wanting a late-night snack. I twisted the key. The lock refused. I took the key out, gave it scrutiny, right key, and tried again with the same result.

Earl Langley, my next-door neighbor, had a spare key but something told me the key wasn't the problem.

I needed to call the night super, but I had no cell phone. It was too late to wake up Earl. Plus, over eighty, he still sometimes kept company. If you know what I mean? But, I really could see no other way.

"Lillian?" He'd thrown on a robe, untied, exposing his striped pajamas. His white hair, what was left, stood up like a crown. His feet, bare.

"I'm so sorry I had to wake you."

He blinked, eyes adjusting. "Can't sleep much at my age. Besides, won't be long and I'll be sleeping all the time." He opened wide the door. "Come in. What do you need? Something wrong?"

I moved inside, explaining, "I can't get into my condo."

"I'll get my key." He started off across to the kitchen. His apartment was a clone of my mother's: living area, kitchen, small hall leading to a bedroom and bath.

"The key won't work." I said, "I need to use your phone. I've...lost mine." I decided not to go into detail.

He looked perplexed. "Sure. It's on the table next to the couch."

I walked into the living space. Couch, recliner, two club chairs, a small television. Remnants of a welcomed nightly "visitor" showed in the half-plate of chocolate chip cookies covered in saran wrap.

Was she still here? Better not to ask.

I found the phone and dialed the super's number. Lake View keeps a super on staff twenty-four hours. Albert Coff worked days, and Jimmy Perkins pulled the night shift. Jimmy was a student at John Adams Community College.

Most residents waited to call in the morning to have Albert sort out their leaky sinks, dripping faucets or backed-up toilets because Jimmy wasn't very handy. But it was a good job for a young kid needing tuition money and time to do his homework.

He was also responsible for calling an ambulance should one be needed. Living in a senior residential complex, a rush to the hospital wasn't unheard of.

It took several rings before he answered. "Hi Jimmy, this is Lillian Dove in number three-o-three. I can't get into my apartment."

There was no response?

"Jimmy, are you awake?"

"Yeah, I'm awake." His voice sounded sleepy. Slow. Hesitant. "How are you calling me if you can't get in?"

"I'm calling from Earl Langley's place."

"Oh. Yeah. Albert told me you might be calling." His voice struggled. "The lock was changed."

"I didn't ask for the lock to be changed." Had someone lost their keys and Albert mistook which condo? It wasn't like Albert to make such a mistake.

Jimmy said, "You should probably talk to Albert."

"It's past midnight. I'm not going to wake Albert. Just bring me the new key. I'll sort this out in the morning."

"Can't."

"What do you mean, can't? Why not?"

Fatigue hit me. The trip to Davenport. Kenny. Iowa State Patrol. Store burglarized. Now, this?

Really, enough was enough.

"Maybe I should get Albert to call you."

"If you don't bring me a key in about two minutes, I'm going to..." I caught myself. None of this was Jimmy's fault and he didn't deserve my wrath at my life always handing me a bum deal.

"Your mother changed the lock."

"My mother?" That couldn't be right. Could it? "Give me Albert's phone number, right now."

I wasn't sure Albert would appreciate him giving me his personal number, but Jimmy did it readily. At his age, I probably would have given it over, too. He hadn't changed the lock, why would he want to take the heat.

I caught Earl up on what was happening. "Paul says Albert put in a new lock."

Earl scratched his bald spot. Yawn.

I let the phone ring. "He had no right to change the locks."

"Didn't he leave you a note?" He went over to one of the club chairs and sat down. "The lock must have been broken."

"Hello?" If Albert listened to Dahlia, then he deserved to lose as much sleep as I was. "Lillian?"

"How'd you know it was me?"

"Jimmy called."

"Then you told him to bring me the key?"

"Can't Lillian. I was told no one else was to get a key."

"Who told you?" Although, I already knew the answer.

"Mrs. Dove called me this morning and ordered the lock changed." He offered the excuse almost as sheepishly as Jimmy. "I suggested she wait until I talked to you about it first, but..." He paused. "She didn't take kindly to my suggestion."

"Sorry, Albert."

"She's the owner. She went ahead and hired Roth's Hardware to come and exchange the lock."

Hadn't Marilyn got ahold of the doctor soon enough to retract his "healthy" diagnosis? Couldn't they have given her something to stop her?

I was going to have a word with Roth's Hardware.

"Lillian, there was nothing I could do."

I apologized for waking him up, asked to tell Jimmy the same when he talked to him, and I tried to reassure him he was not to blame.

"I'll get this all straightened out in the morning."

Tomorrow things will be back to normal, the whisper beside me said.

CHAPTER THIRTEEN

M y credit card wouldn't hold much more, so a motel room was out of the question. I had another set of keys in my purse, attached to the same key ring as Discount, Clarence's house.

Clarence Salzman believed in me when I couldn't believe in myself. He saw something in me no one else did. He left me not only AAA Discount Liquor but also his house on Church Street.

I drove the Mustang into the driveway. Got out of the car. I headed to the porch, then stopped. More than anything, I wanted to go in, fall into bed, and sleep the night away. Only I couldn't move forward. I'd worked at the store part-time for five years. What I truly knew about Clarence I could have listed on a Post-It note: unmarried, told jokes, maybe had trouble in his life. I think he guessed I had a past, but he never asked. What he knew about my life was DahIf life is one big bowl of cherries, why was I so addicted to chocolate?

I leaned against the car, unwrapped the bar half down, careful to save the wrapping in case I only binged part way, and nibbled, letting a soft piece of chocolate melt on my tongue.

Our house in New Liberty had a porch. Its front door was painted black, just like this one. Was that what bothered me? Did Clarence's house remind me too much of my childhood home? Dalia. — *Ain't no point in beatin' a dead horse...'course, can't hurt none either. Only, your mother, Lillian, is still alive.*

I could write a whole book about Dahlia. Cover to cover. Maybe more than one.

I needed a Snickers. I went to the car, opened the glove box and pulled out one of the two chocolate bars I kept for emergencies. How did the State Patrol miss these?

If life is one big bowl of cherries, why was I so addicted to chocolate?

I leaned against the car, unwrapped the bar half down, careful to save the wrapping in case I only binged part way, and nibbled, letting a soft piece of chocolate melt on my tongue.

Our house in New Liberty had a porch. Its front door was painted black, just like this one. Was that what bothered me? Did Clarence's house remind me too much of my childhood home?

I gnawed off a bigger bite, gooey caramel, peanuts, and chocolate.

Hell, I wasn't a child any longer. I'd changed. This was my house now, *not Dahlia's*. I could create something new. Like I created a new life in Frytown.

I ripped off the brown wrapping. *Mine!* I began gobbling the Snickers, wolfing it down like it was my last meal.

If I went out to Charles's place, he'd let me stay. I thought back to the first night when I'd accepted a dinner invitation and stormy weather moved us to his bed, our passion as robust and divine as the thunder booming. But while some storms clean the air and offer new beginnings, storms can also meander, building up too great a pressure. I lost my job at the FPD. I became an eyewitness to arson and involved Dahlia in something which almost got both of us murdered. I'd let myself become vulnerable.

Even if I kept to Charles's couch and didn't let myself surrender to his arms, I would still believe it was he keeping me safe.

I needed to learn to trust me.

Besides, I was already in a pile of trouble. I was locked out of the condo. I had Kenny Liky after me. And he seemed senselessly desperate. Who knows, maybe he had more than a lieutenant out to get me.

Was that even possible?

My certainty in where my life was heading was as unsatisfying as the first Snickers. I reached and took out the other bar, telling myself as soon as I finished it, I'd go on inside.

I devoured the second bar in chunks, and although each bite became harder and harder to swallow, I craved its sweetness, the calming caramel running through the crunchy peanuts. I fancied the chocolate would make me feel better. I always do. Yet, I felt sick when I finished.

I suppose life is full of desire for something different. Too bad we don't come into life with a "How To" manual.

I got back into the car and retraced my route back to Lake View. Wrapping my jacket around me, I curled into the backseat and shivered myself to sleep.

As soon as I closed my eyes, I breathed in the smell of algae, dust and the leavings of small animals. I was on the island.

I wasn't lost. I'd been on this island before, but I thought I'd escaped this dream. My sleep hadn't been disturbed in months.

All horizons still offered cold, grey water. Yet, unlike other dreams, this one provided a closer horizon. I could see a hint of something. A building? City? Could I swim that far? Brush surrounded me. There lay a wilderness to push through.

In my last dream, I'd seen Cressie. And Clarence? Yes, he'd been with her. Were they still just on the other side? If I pushed through, would I find them?

"I doubt you'll get there in my lifetime." Dahlia manifested before me. In her hand, she held a skeleton key. "No, sir," she goaded. "Not as long as I got the key."

"Unlock the door," I ordered her. How dare she lock me out of my house.

"Not yours, mine." She laughed and dangled the key like a feather strung on a pole.

I jumped. "You had no right." My fingertips touched metal.

She jerked the key out of my reach. I jumped again.

She cackled, "I'm fit as a fiddle. The doctor said so." She jiggled the key, and I rallied myself to reach it this time. Jerk it out of her hands. But faster than I could spring up, her lips parted. She raised the key over the dark hole of her mouth, holding it as she might a salty sardine taken from a can. She glanced over, winked, then let it drop. Swallowed.

"No!" I screamed.

She grinned, "Can't kill me."

CHAPTER FOURTEEN   YOU DIDN'T DO IT
OCTOBER 31ST, FRIDAY, AM

S c r e a m -
ing.

I opened my eyes.

I heard a low, rumbling hum, sounding like large engines. Voices called out to one another. I got out and walked around the parking structure to the front entrance of the building. Police cars were parked willy-nilly along the curb, others blocked the street. A fire engine stood double-parked, firefighters at the ready. Behind the engine was a paramedic van, back doors winged open.

Officer Garth Davis stood at the front entrance. He waved me over. When I got closer, he said, "Man, did someone put a curse on you?"

I would have laughed if he hadn't been so damn serious. "Leveque's put an APB out on you?"

"For what?" Did Leveque think I ruined my own business for the insurance money?

"You'd better get inside."

Paramedics standing in the corridor half-leaned on an empty gurney. A crowd of officers grouped around them. They were all watching the opened door to my condo.

Miner broke from the crowd. "Where have you been?" He took my elbow, leading me through the open doorway. I glanced to the left and saw Nelly Crow. Her pirate costume had been changed to a skirt and blouse, a white netted cap pinned reverently on her head. Seeing me, she anxiously glanced across the room.

Dahlia sat in her wheelchair. "You've done it this time, girlie," she called out, shoulders hunkering down, lips smacking together with contempt.

My nose itched from a scent my memory told me I'd smelled before, but I couldn't quite put my finger on what it was.

Still not fully awake, I tried to take in the scene. The living room had been ransacked. The room matched the upheaval of the store. Had the person who burglarized it come here? But how did they know where I lived?

Cushions, pillows, and knick-knacks littered the floor. Gutted paper hung out from desk drawers. On top of the desk, my computer illuminated ribbons of color crisscrossing its screen. Someone had turned it on.

"Where the hell was she?" His voice hit me, and I twisted around at its impact. Leveque charged out of the kitchen. Wearing jeans, a shirt, and a leather jacket, his badge was clipped noticeably to his shirt.

I disregarded him, dark-cherry-colored tracks on the carpet taking my notice. They came from the kitchen. They looked like thin wheels. Dahlia? Wheelchair? Had she done something to Bacardi? She hated cats. Any animals, for that matter. She never allowed us kids pets, and said she didn't need another mouth to feed.

"Where were you?" he barked.

Why was he barking at me? What the hell had gone on here?

But paramedics wouldn't be called for a cat. Had someone thought she'd run over me?

In a haze of trying to connect the dots with all that had happened in the past twenty-four hours, I gave him a truthful answer. "I was asleep in my car."

Charles came out of the kitchen. "Slept in your car? I dropped you off last night at about midnight. Why were you in your car?" He was dressed in uniform and was wearing disposable gloves. His voice was insistent, but his tone was even-keeled.

I glanced at Leveque's hands. He was also wearing gloves.

"Lil," Charles called, grabbing my attention again. "I thought you came home to go to bed."

Davenport, blackmail, Candlelight, Kenny, Cressie dead? Charles, paramedics. Dahlia, alive? Empty gurney. Leveque,? APB? No connections. My mind was spinning.

While Charles and I have a "past", however short, he keeps business and personal separate. "I was going to," I began explaining, "but I figured I wouldn't be able to sleep, so I went back to the store to start cleaning up."

"That still doesn't explain sleeping in your car?" Leveque snapped.

Okay, I wasn't appreciating Leveque's adversity. After all, why was he so wound up? It wasn't his store that had been ransacked. His condo had been torn up. His mother was a pain in the backside.

I ignored him and said to Charles, "I tried to clean up, but it was too hard. Everything's ruined. So I came back, and I was going to go to bed and try to face it all later. But I couldn't get in."

"What time was that?" Charles questioned.

At the same time, Leveque growled, "You expect us to believe that?"

Leveque might be wearing a shield, but his tone definitely told everyone within hearing distance that he didn't like me. The reason wasn't only because I refused his unsubtle advances or because Charles negated his own policy of officers not fraternizing with staff. I'd stepped on his toes with the arson case last summer by proving I was right. Edgar Pike was the horrible, murderous man I'd thought he was. I just hadn't put together the other person involved. But neither had Leveque.

My upping him took him down a peg with the other guys at the station. Flattened his ego. After all, he was the detective.

Charles wasn't addressing Leveque's tone because whatever happened would become Leveque's case. And while I didn't hold his abilities to any professional level, Charles never once showed anything but a high regard for Leveque's investigative talents.

"I'm not sure of the time," I said to both. "Maybe an hour later. About one?" I had questions of my own and changed the subject from me. "Did the same person who broke into the store do this?"

"Maybe you can tell us," Charles said. He began to back-step into the kitchen.

Leveque stopped me from following him. "Why couldn't you get in?"

Did he think I was lying? Did he think I came into my own place, and tossed it, just to ruin his day? Yeah, he would. Leveque would just love to hear how my own mother locked me out of the place where I'd been living.

I told Charles, "The locks had been changed."

Leveque's next question dumbfounded me. "If you couldn't get in, then how did he get in?"

My eyes went again to the dark red tracks. He wasn't talking about Bacardi.

At that very moment, Dale Buck, coroner for Frytown, came out of the kitchen. Leveque and Charles went over to him. I caught fragments of their conversation, "lividity," "six to eight hours."

"I'll walk you out, Dale." Charles gave me a "don't worry" smile and said to Leveque. "I'll be outside if you need me."

My security blanket was being led away.

As soon as Charles was gone, Leveque moved purposefully back to me. "So far, nothing you're saying is adding up? You'd better start explaining, and fast." He headed inside the kitchen, paused, staring at me as if waiting for me to follow him, and then moved to the side of the doorway at my invitation.

I choked in seeing the dark tracks on the carpet transform into a bright red on the white linoleum floor where lay a man's lifeless body. His eyes bulged, mouth open. His tawny brown hair was matted, wet, and red, darker on the back of his head. And something else, in his hair and in the puddle where his head lay, a grey curdled matter.

"I'm going to be sick." My legs went limp. My stomach did a loop-t-loop and fell to my bowels. I retched.

"Don't you dare puke on my crime scene." Leveque jerked me upright. He pointed. "Who is this?"

He was still wearing the blue flannel jacket. Keds.

"Kenny."

"Do you have a last name?"

"Liky."

"You know him?"

Again, my stomach looped. I turned my head away but not without catching sight of the red paw prints moving across the white linoleum floor to an upturned food bowl, kibble scattered.

Leveque stood inches from my ear. "Where have you been in the last six hours?"

"Get out of the way." I pushed him aside.

I ran into the bathroom. Having not eaten for almost twenty-four hours, there was little in my stomach. I heaved and retched yellow phlegm.

Someone squeezed my shoulders. Rubbed. "Are you all right, Lillian?" It was Nelly.

"No." I was suddenly cold. "Yes." Freezing.

"Is he a friend of yours? We found him when we got here this morning." She got no further in her explanation.

"Get it together, Lillian," Leveque ordered.

I heaved again. Laid my head on the toilet seat and glanced back and saw Leveque squared in the doorway. His curly hair was longer than regulation, the back coming just short of his jacket collar, but Detective Jacque Leveque didn't always hold to the rules. His voice lowered, yet still a hint of a growl. "Tell me again, where you were?"

Surely he didn't think I'd done this. "I told you. I was sleeping in my car."

I went to get up, and as I did, the image of Kenny flashed in my mind, and again my legs weakened. But I was damned if I was going to sit at a toilet bowl with Leveque bearing over me.

"Are you sure you're okay?" Nelly asked.

No, I wasn't sure. I nodded. "Thanks, Nelly."

At her leaving, I took a deep breath. Steadied myself. I moved over towards when Leveque stood, saying calmly, rationally, "The locks had been changed, so I slept out in the garage in my car."

I'm not sure it was the confident tone of my voice or my breath that made him take two steps back. I also didn't care which. "When the sirens woke me, I thought something happened to my mother. She has a weak heart."

He spat back, "Why did you think your mother would be here?"

I returned his irritable glare, hoping mine projected the same annoyed countenance. "Dahlia's as bullheaded as they get. She got it into her mind that she was *good as new*. She thinks she's moving back in."

He rubbed his forehead, moving his fingers through his dark curls. He glanced over his shoulder toward the living room, then asked, "That still doesn't explain why would she have changed the locks."

"Exactly." Point made.

He shook his head and stepped into the corridor. I took the opportunity to move past him. "Has anyone seen my cat?"

"Miner," Leveque barked, following me. "Check the parking structure. Find Lillian's junk of a car. No one's to go near it until forensics gets here. And I want the entire area taped off, both the parking structure and entrances. No one comes or leaves without being escorted until the investigation's finished."

Without losing a measured beat, he returned his agitation back to me. His voice dripping with sarcasm. "You want me to believe this story?"

"I don't care what you believe, Leveque. Ask Garth. He saw me coming from that direction."

He ignored the suggestion. "Can you explain then why the door wasn't locked when your mother and Ms. Crow got here? They stated the door was open."

What was he implying? I made a logical guess. "Someone broke in."

"No signs of a break-in," he returned.

I searched for Dahlia, finding her in the same place as when I first entered, only this time, she sat a little higher in her chair, intrigued with the drama going on around her.

As if she'd been given her cue, she called for Nelly's assistance. Nelly and she exchanged words. Nelly shook her head. Dahlia put her hands on the chair's wheels and began to move forward. Knowing she was probably incapable of stopping her, Nelly got behind her chair and maneuvered it through the scatter on the floor.

As soon as she was close, I directed Dahlia to tell Leveque she'd changed the locks so I couldn't get in. If Leveque was ridiculous enough to believe I had something to do with Kenny's death, I needed to set him straight.

He respectfully squatted next to Dahlia's wheelchair so he could be on an equal eye level. His voice changed to a softened, subdued tone. "You must be very upset by all of this, Mrs. Dove, but it would be helpful if you can confirm whether your daughter had access to this condo between the hours of ten last night and eight this morning. I would also like you to reconfirm that the door was open when you arrived."

She tilted her head slightly, eyes cowed, and in a small, quiet voice, she said, "I never saw someone dead before." She grimaced. "Except for my husband, of course."

Dahlia was a little bothered about anything in life. And why would she bring my father into the conversation? She made it sound as if he'd been found in a comparable situation. My father died in a hospital from cirrhosis of the liver.

"I'm sorry for your loss," Leveque quickly apologized. Dahlia gave him such a feeble, hurt, grieving expression, anyone watching would think she was a vulnerable widow. "If I can, I have a couple more questions for you, and then you can return with Ms. Crow back to the home."

She blinked. "Home?" Her expression soured. She pursed her lips. "I am at home."

Leveque said patiently, "I meant, I'll let you go back to where you've been living. You won't want to stay here. Not after this." He reached out and put his hand on top of hers.

The move might have been received as a sign of sympathetic affection. By anyone other than Dahlia.

She jerked her hand out from beneath his. "Don't be telling me what I want and what I don't want. I have a mind of my own."

"Of course you do." Leveque looked quizzically at Nelly, as if not understanding how he'd warranted the reaction.

Nelly immediately tried to appease both parties. "The police are not going to let you move back in now, Dahlia. Not until they figure out what happened."

Dahlia's lips smacked together.

"That's what I meant," Leveque corrected himself, seeming grateful for having himself clarified. "The investigation is going to take a couple of days. And you'll want to have a cleaning company come in." He paused and looked helplessly at Nelly as if seeking whether his mentioning the cleaning of the kitchen might have been too much for her elderly charge.

Again Nelly offered her assistance by suggesting to Dahlia how she would bring her back to the condo as soon as the police gave word. But I knew Nelly. She was only making the gesture as a means of getting Dahlia to leave. When they got back to Oaks, Nelly would use what happened as the reason why it wasn't safe for Dahlia to come back to the condo to live. She'd remind Dahlia how lucky she was that the person hadn't broken in while she was living by herself. And, how she needed to stay living where she was.

Leveque must have felt he was on safer ground. "Can you affirm your daughter hasn't been able to get into the condo?"

Single-minded, Dahlia grabbed both arms of her chair. "I'm going to stay right here."

As if she had senior dementia, he hinted again at what was in the kitchen. "You won't be able to take possession until the investigation is closed. That will be at least a couple of days."

"Don't be telling me what I can and cannot do." She twisted around. "Nelly, get a mop. We'll do some cleaning up right now." She almost knocked Leveque on his butt as she grabbed her wheels and rolled in my direction, stopping right in front of me. "Lillian?" She scooted to the edge of her chair as if she was going to stand, put her hands on her knees, pushing herself up slightly, almost rising out, as she said, "What did you do?"

"Me? You were here before me," I threw back. "What did you do?"

She sat heavy with a grunt. Shook her head. "You've been trouble since the day you were born."

A small stab, one I'd heard many times. I tried to amend the state of affairs. "You can't stay here right now. Go back with Nelly."

She grunted angrily.

I added, "Then we'll talk about you coming here to live."

"I'm done talking."

"Okay, move in if you want." I acquiesced.

A triumphant smile bloomed on her lips.

I bribed, "I won't try to stop you...if you tell Officer Leveque..."

"Detective Leveque," he interrupted. He hated that I never called him by his official title.

"Tell Officer Leveque you changed the locks yesterday. Tell him I couldn't have got into the condo."

She frowned. "Well, I sure as heck didn't let the man in. Who else would he come to see?" With that said, she abruptly swiveled her chair around, saying to Leveque as if they held the same opinion of me, "She's always getting her nose into things where it doesn't belong."

Leveque seemed to have been watching the interaction between Dahlia and me with a whole new expression. Implausible? Unreal? Flabbergasted was probably a better word for his stunned, wide-eyed stare.

I moved around Dalhia, telling Nelly, "Take her back. I'll try to stop by later today."

Nelly took hold of the chair. "Come on, Mrs. Dove. If they need to ask more questions, they can find you at Oaks Manor."

"Nelly," Dahlia ordered her. "You let go of this chair"

However, Nelly began wheeling her away. Then stopped. She said to Leveque, "Detective. Mrs. Dove had the locks changed. It was all she could talk about on her way over here. She kept saying how Lillian must have got the shock of her life when she couldn't get in last night."

Nelly's desertion to the other side raised Dahlia's ire beyond being forced to leave. "Nelly, I don't need you telling tales."

Nelly continued. "I can also affirm the door was unlatched when we got here. Not completely open, more like someone didn't make sure it was securely closed."

'Thank you." I was truly grateful Nelly offered the truth and offered her a look of sympathy, for I knew the risk she was taking. After all, she was going to be in the car with Dahlia driving back to Oaks, and Dahlia would probably vent her anger on both Nelly and me on others at the home.

She was already shouting, "Nelly, turn my chair around. You leave me be. You hear?"

But Nelly continued rolling her out of the condo, her own lips stubbornly set.

I said to Leveque, "Last time I saw Kenny Liky was when I met him in Davenport yesterday evening."

But Leveque was still looking toward the open door and the corridor where we could hear Dahlia shouting, "Stop her, one of you. She's kidnapping me."

He absently mindedly asked, "Time?"

"I want her arrested." Dahlia's voice, loud and clear.

"Around seven. I checked out of the Radisson around nine."

Paramedics came through the doorway bringing in the gurney. Their appearance broke Leveque's notice of what was going on in the corridor and brought him back to his line of questioning. "Then you more than just knew him?"

I didn't like his suggestion and ignored the implication. "We met at a restaurant. We argued, and I left."

"Argued about what?"

That was as far as I was going to go at the moment. I didn't want to delve into why Kenny and I met. Not until I knew why he'd shown up in my condo, dead. Plus, I didn't like Leveque's suggestion Kenny and I had an intimate relationship.

"Stop her," Dahlia still ordering.

The paramedics exited the kitchen, this time with the bagged body of Kenny Liky lying on top.

Moving to the kitchen doorway, I could see the counter. Nothing was amiss. There was the glass I'd last used. The coffee container. Bacardi's kibble box.

Where was Bacardi? Had the person who done this harmed him, too? Had he escaped from the door left open?

My mind took in how the room was still neat and tidy in contrast to the rest of the house.

Leveque pulled a small pad out of his pocket. He began writing, asked. "Why does your mother think you were involved?"

It would take a lot longer than this investigation to answer that question. I'd spent most of my life wondering why Dahlia thought I was bungling and useless. Her questioning indication I could have killed someone was new on her pathetic-Lillian list.

"I pay your paycheck, don't you know?" Nelly hadn't gotten too far. I envisioned Dahlia's hands on the chair's wheels, trying to turn back what Nelly was moving forward.

I turned around and went to the corridor. Poor Nelly, Dahlia was my responsibility, not hers.

Dahlia had grabbed Officer Dave Richard's leg. Nelly was bent over, trying to pry Dahlia's fingers away. And Richards, face beet red, seemed to be looking everywhere but at the two women, his eyes seeking help from any one of the other officers holding their stomachs, trying to keep from falling down on the floor laughing.

There was nothing else to do. "Dahlia quit. Go back with Nelly. I'll come over as soon as I can."

She returned a bitter mouthful, but I didn't catch it.

"Take your hands off this poor officer. He's done nothing to you to warrant this abuse."

She glanced at me, frowned, and then looked up as if she'd forgotten she was holding onto a leg and not a post. "I don't want to go," she told him.

Officer Richards nodded to me, then said to her. "Would you like me to escort you out to your car?"

I expected a "hell no", but Dahlia smiled at the idea.

"Here, ma'am." He took Nelly's place behind the chair.

Ah, a man in uniform. Dahlia twisted around and gave him the type of smile a six-teen-year-old girl might.

Nelly slumped with the drain on her patience, gave me a weak smile, and followed the Richards and Dahlia out of the building. His offer just might have made Nelly's ride home a small, bit better.

Once Dahlia's mulish stalemate, the corridor became quiet. Eyes were on me as I went back to the condo. Whatever they thinking? "Boy, no wonder she's like she is with a mother like that?"

Leveque had witnessed the whole scene. He smiled like a Halloween pumpkin, and said, "I can see where you get it."

CHAPTER FIFTEEN

I'd worked at the police station, so I was familiar with the interrogation room. A small station, with few real criminals, the room was small, painted white, with a table and three chairs. It never seemed so stifling when I would come in to sit to have a peaceful cup of coffee at the end of my shift. But with Leveque sitting across from me, the room shrank to miniature.

Slightly damp from sweat, his dark curly hair tumbled onto his forehead.

"Where's the Chief, Leveque? I want to see Charles."

While waiting for Charles and Leveque, I ran all the events through my mind over and over again. Someone had planted heroin on me. The patrol officer, if he had been a real lieutenant, stopped me to look for it. Why? To arrest me? Or to threaten me?

It had to be Kenny. The officer must have been a friend of his. A put-up to get me scared and more willing to his blackmail

Did Kenny also have someone bust up Discount? But, if he had, why did he come back and break into my place?

And who had been following him? Apparently, not one of his friends.

I didn't know how long I'd been answering questions, but it seemed like hours.

When Leveque came in, he'd placed a tape recorder on the table. I knew the security camera above the door was also recording.

"Let's go over this one more time." He raised his arms in a stretch as if he had all day while I repeated the same thing over and over again. He said, "Start this time coming back from the store after the Chief dropped you off."

I hadn't resisted coming to the station. After all, there was a man dead in the kitchen where I'd lived for the last five years. I knew the dead man. In fact, I'd just seen him a few hours prior.

Routine questions, Leveque had said. Of course, I knew when someone was brought to the station, it was never without purpose. But I figured Charles would be there, too.

Only, so far, I hadn't seen Charles. Was he standing behind the two-way window? If he didn't step inside pretty soon, I was going to ask to call for a lawyer. The questions were becoming more threatening.

I placed my palms flat on the table, fingers spread wide. Nothing to hide. I wanted to yawn but stifled it, overhearing Leveque once telling Garth Davis that people who are guilty generally fall asleep while they wait for questioning. Or, they can hardly keep their eyes open during an interrogation. He said it was an unconscious sign of guilt. The arrest acted as a relief from the worry of being caught.

I sat purposefully at attention all the while, eyes open. Only now, letting my weight lean on my hands, my body drained from the lack of a good night's sleep and the stress of finding my life quickly unraveling. My voice sounded tired, offering an airy quality. "For the *third* time. After coming back to the condo, I decided to go back to Discount to clean up."

"You didn't go into the condo? Don't you think that's a bit strange? I'd think you'd want to pull yourself together or verify everything was all right there, first."

My voice reflected my overall aggravation with all these repeated scenarios. "Again, I didn't need to go inside, as you say, to pull myself together. I wasn't worried about making sure everything was all right. When I left that morning, everything was fine, and there was nothing to tell me any different. My concern was whether there was enough inventory left for me to stay in business." And I added because it was true, "I was worried about Percy."

"Did Chief Kaefring come into the condo building with you?"

Another imagined setup to confuse me.

"As I said," my voice rising, "Chief Kaefring followed me home from the store wanting to make sure I got in and was safe. He did not come in."

"How did he know you were safe, then?"

"I waved from outside to let him know I was all right and for him to go on."

"Why didn't he come inside with you? He's been inside before, hasn't he?"

I knew what he was insinuating, but I refused to go there.

He shocked me by saying, "I apologize. I meant nothing by the question."

Yeah sure. He only apologized because we were being recorded. Charles was listening.

Only, with his next question, his tone changed completely. "Wouldn't you not going in sound strange to you if you were in my position?" He gave a thoughtful expression. "You have to admit, it sounds strange to have gone back to the store. It may not have been safe."

He came to his conclusion. "Plus, I'd think you'd have been exhausted after everything that occurred."

"I was. But I knew I wouldn't be able to go to sleep."

He became thoughtful.

I reaffirmed. "I went straight back to the store."

He nodded. "Did you see any unusual cars parked on the street when you left?"

"I told you, I didn't look. I wasn't expecting anyone."

"How long were you at the store?"

I gave an exasperated sigh. "Again. Half hour. Maybe an hour. I swept some of the broken glass. Saved what snacks I could. I told you, Leveque, whoever did this to my store took me out of business. Everything Clarence built has been ruined."

"And you have no idea who would want to do this to you?"

"No."

He got up out of his chair. I thought we were done.

He pushed his chair into the table, hard. The sound vibrated off the walls, causing me to jump. "You expect me to believe you have no idea who or why someone broke into your liquor store? You expect me to believe a man you said you met in Davenport followed you back to Frytown, for no apparent reason? This man ended up in the condo, where you were living, coincidentally, and ended up with a bullet in his head, execution-style? Not the fate of robbers.

He stopped. Stared. "I'll tell you what I believe, Lillian. I believe there's something you're not telling me."

He moved around the table, dragging his empty chair behind him, its legs scraping the floor like fingernails on a blackboard. He hiked his foot on the chair's seat, crossed his arms on his knee, and leaned over so close I could smell a musky scent of adrenaline beneath the cologne he'd bathed in. He held the position for several seconds before smiling flirtatiously. Then he immediately smirked, "Where's the gun Clarence kept in the store?"

It was a new question, and asking it threw me off-guard.

He banged his fist on the table. "Don't think. Tell me. Where is it?"

I hiccupped. "In the store beneath the cash drawer."

He stepped off the chair, shoving it away with his foot. It toppled over with a bang. He came and grabbed the back of my chair with one hand, curling himself around me by placing his other hand on the table. He was so close, I had to remind myself to breathe, and yet, when I did breathe, I hiccupped.

"I had the store searched. There is no gun."

"What? No. Ask Charles. He asked about it last night. It was there."

Had Charles told him Clarence kept a gun at the store? Did they think it was the gun that killed Kenny?

"You're saying you showed the gun to the Chief?"

"No, but I told him it was there."

"But he didn't see it?"

I remembered bending down to verify it was in its place beneath the cash drawer. But, did I see it? Or did I just think it was where it should have been? I shook my head.

"Then you lied?"

I hiccupped.

"Lillian Dove, did you kill the man found in the kitchen of the condo where you have been living?"

"No."

He hit the table with his fist. He was so close, the sound hit me. He spun the questioning away from the gun. "Why did you go to Davenport? Why did Mr. Liky follow you to Frytown?"

If I told him or Charles now that Kenny had tried blackmailing me for killing Cressie, it would give me a really big motive for killing him.

I stood. I needed time to think.

"Sit down."

"Are you placing me under arrest? If so, I want to call a lawyer." I didn't exactly have a lawyer, except for one I would find in the yellow pages.

His approach immediately changed. He backed up, holding his arms out to his sides. "Take it easy. We're merely having a discussion about what occurred. And while it may not seem like it right now, I'm trying to help you." He went over and got his chair, put it back into position at the table, and sat down, leaning back, relaxed.

I didn't return to my chair. I walked over to the one-way window. I addressed Charles. "I learned a few things while working here. The first is that I don't need to answer any questions unless charges are being filed against me. If I haven't been placed under arrest, I know what I say before Miranda rights *can* be used against me in a court of law."

"Lillian," Leveque called. "Come on. Let's talk."

I jerked around, hiccups gone. "We're done."

CHAPTER SIXTEEN

W hen I walked out and down the hall to the lobby of the station, I was surprised to find Lieutenant Manville, Officer Mitch Miner, and Donna Stockman standing at the window. Not Charles.

Donna said, "I don't believe a word of this, Lillian."

"Please find Bacardi, Donna. I think he's been let out."

I continued, not wanting Leveque to have time to reconsider some obscure charge he could place on me.

I stopped at Charles's glassed-section area, thinking I'd go and complain about Leveque's treatment. Only I saw Mayor Johns pacing in front of the Chief's assistant's desk.

The mayor's arms were swinging as if to ward off everything thrown at him by the public and the media. Peggy, the Chief's assistant, and a fellow Frytown gossiper, was giving him her undivided attention. Then Councilman Pane came out of Charles's office along with Charles. They walked over to someone else who was listening to Mayor Johns. He was leaning on the corner of Peggy's desk with his back to me.

"Lillian? We're not done here."

Hearing my name called, Charles glanced in my direction. The man sitting on the corner of Peggy's desk also turned around. I didn't recognize him.

Checking over my shoulder, I saw Leveque coming toward me with what appeared to be full, angered intent on dragging me back into the interrogation room. I hurried on, past cubicles with officers at their desks. Officer Richards broke off a conversation on the telephone to look up and see what was going on. Officer Stiller, stood, maybe unsure whether he needed to stop me or not. Before he heard Leveque and decided it may be the appropriate action, I opened the door to the lobby and continued moving purposefully past the counter where I once sat answering phones.

CHAPTER SEVENTEEN

I t didn't occur to me until I was on the sidewalk that I didn't have a car.

Glancing toward the 218 Highway exit and the Gas for Less station, I saw Percy's truck parked alongside the building. I doubted he was there, but if his nephew Pete had the truck, I'd get him to give me a ride back to my car.

It was, at least, a half-mile.

I headed out, expecting at any point to hear a car come up behind me, and Leveque jumping out.

CHAPTER EIGHTEEN

"I f it's not running, I'll take a look at it," Pete offered after pulling up to the curb in front of Lake View.

I'd told him my car wouldn't start and that it was probably out of gas. He insisted he brings along a gallon container, enough to get me back out to the station.

Immediately I noticed the space where I parked my car was empty. I knew Leveque impounded it, but I hadn't thought they'd have taken it, yet.

I told Pete, "Come to think of it, I just put gas in it yesterday. It should have plenty of gas."

He looked a bit confused. Me, too.

"The robbery at the store has got me pretty shooken. The transmission must be giving me trouble again. Why don't I have Percy take a look at it in a couple of days when he's feeling better."

"I can take a look now." He offered.

"Ah, Percy's pretty protective of me. He'll want to check it even if you get it running. Why don't we just wait? In fact, if you could drop me off at Discount, instead, that would really help out."

"You sure? I'm getting as good as my uncle. Just ask him."

"It's really important for me to get to the store as soon as possible."

"It might not take long."

"Please, Pete." I wanted to go back and see if Clarence's gun was where it should be. Or had the police taken it? Was it the gun used to kill Kenny?

"But then how will you get home?"

"I'll have a friend pick me up." Friend? Donna. We needed to find Bacardi. The condo would be taped off until forensics was complete. But, she might be able to get me inside. I was sure Charles would let me in to get some clothes.

I thought again about Bacardi and his paw prints in Kenny's blood. If he was still in the condo, he was probably hiding beneath the bed.

When we got to Discount, my plans changed again. A patrol car was parked in the parking lot. Now, what to do?

"Hey, if you need transportation, you can use this truck. I know Percy'd be okay with me lending it to you. As I said, he ain't going to be needing it. He's not allowed to drive for a couple of weeks."

"But you're using it. I couldn't put you out."

"Ah, hell, I don't need it."

He was wearing overalls from working on a car at the station, old grease stains on the knees, but newly washed. His face was smooth, with barely a hint of a mustache he was trying to grow. Brown hair cut and combed decent. He had long dark lashes over green, hazel eyes. He said, "I got friends that'll take me where I need to get."

Maybe he was feeling bad about being late to pick Percy up at the store. Maybe he was thinking if he'd been on time, the burglary would never have occurred.

The idea of using the truck gave me another idea. I was sure Donna would check on Percy. I had other things I needed to check on.

"We should ask Percy first."

"Sure." He pulled out his cell phone, thumb punching in numbers. He handed the phone to me.

I asked Percy how he was doing.

"Sore as hell, but I'm gonna live. I'll be able to help you with things tomorrow."

"Pete told me you aren't supposed to drive for two weeks. You just stay put. In fact, I was calling you to see if I could borrow your truck for a couple of days. My car's not working, and Pete says he has friends that'll take him to work."

"I'll tell Petey to take a look at it."

I glanced over at Pete. I knew my next words were going to hurt him. "I'd rather have you.",

"Okay. But you need to get yourself a better car." He asked, "You get those new tires as I told you?"

"No. I'll take you with me when I go to get them."

"As soon as I'm able, we need to go get them, Lillian. You should at least get a spare."

"I know. But you know how it is. Money disappears like a good beer."

He laughed. "You can say that twice."

"And with the store..." I stopped. He became quiet. I didn't mean to imply anything.

He said. "I'll have Pete take a look at your car. He can call me with what he sees. Let me talk to Pete."

"Really, I can wait for you to fix the car. After today, I'm not going to even need this truck." I didn't want to explain to Percy why the police impounded the Mustang. "I just need to handle a couple of things today. Then I'm going to take some time off until all this gets figured out."

"Okay, let me talk to Petey. He's kind of in the dog house at the moment, and I want to give him the rules of having his friends run him around."

I handed Pete his phone. I wondered if his being in the dog house had anything to do with what happened at the store."

"I know. I won't." Whatever Percy was saying caused the red in Pete's face to weep down his neck. "I said I won't. I'll get Mom or Benny to give me a lift." He turned his head to look out the side window. He said, softer, "I know." He ended the call. "Percy says for you to take the truck for as long as you need."

"You sure?"

He offered, "I can wait if you need to go inside."

"No. It's okay. Thanks for the truck."

As we passed Discount, I saw Garth in the police car deep in conversation on his cell phone. I wondered who he was talking to. Had he spotted us? Was he checking in with Leveque?

Pete must have noticed the car, too, but he didn't mention it. He was chewing on his cheek, thinking maybe about what Percy had said to him.

CHAPTER NINETEEN

W hen I'd asked Percy why he'd purchased a small Dodge pickup instead of a larger truck, he'd said, "Big enough."

Compared to my Mustang, the truck was not only big enough, but I felt a lot safer behind the wheel as I pulled out onto Highway 218 and headed once more to Davenport.

Like the last trip, I knew I shouldn't be going. Returning to Davenport was definitely a big mistake. If Leveque learned I'd left, he'd use it as a sure sign of guilt, and he'd be after me like a dog after a favorite chew bone.

A shrink might say I was trying to make up for past sins. Kenny's death was sad but expected. He lived the life. But with him went the answers to what happened to Cress

I still felt responsible for her. Responsibility never needs logical reasoning, it merely requires commitment.

Kenny also took with him why he'd come to Frytown, and why doing so caused his murder.

Leveque asked too many questions about the gun at Discount. But he'd also offered how Kenny had died, information not generally shared at the beginning of an investigation. Was his sharing it a slight, or did he know I had nothing to do with the crime? Or at least not with Kenny's death.

Sometimes life seems to be full of more questions than answers.

I supposed, even though the evidence was pointing in my direction at the moment, Leveque believed I couldn't have killed Kenny. I'm not the killing type if there is a type. But he thought I was involved somehow, and that I would lead him to some answers.

I needed to believe I could find answers before more happened to make others think I was guilty or thought Kenny and I were in cahoots.

CHAPTER TWENTY   IS THERE PROOF?

OCTOBER 31ST, FRIDAY, PM

O f course, I had no real plan.

I had no idea where to start looking for answers. I hadn't heard from Kenny in five years. But I'd had a routine and Kenny crossed it most nights, so I figured I'd learn the most by hitting the Candlelight first.

Back on Locust Street. Round and round I go.

The heavy door opened lightly to a bar so dark the bartender served drinks in silhouette. A mirror ran behind the bar doubling the inventory kept at hand. Pour spouts held ready to offer their nectar without spilling a drop. Club glasses were stacked on a working counter, and stemmed glasses hung above.

My old companion stepped in with me. *You'll be okay. You're strong enough.* I gave a shudder and glanced to the back of the room, to the third stool from the wall. Cressie's stool. I wanted her to be sitting on it.

It was two in the afternoon. Those who'd stopped by for a beer and burger were gone. The place was near to empty. Two people sat on the opposite side of the bar from where Cressie and I would sit. The woman giggled as the man sitting next to her refilled her glass from the bottle in front of them. The only other customer was a man lying with his head down on the counter, a glass held loosely in his clasped hands.

I took a seat in my usual place.

The ghost of a bartender came over and wiped the area clean in front of me with his dirty rag. "What can I do you for?"

Nothing was absolute anymore. I turned to the stool next to me. Empty. "Club soda, please, with a twist of lime."

The bartender hadn't changed, but he didn't seem to recognize me. He brought my club soda. I said, "Hi, Bud."

He gave me a good look over. "By God, I thought you looked familiar. Where've you been?"

He may not recall my name, but he hadn't lost my face. "I got sober."

"Happens to the best of us." He chuckled.

"Hey, Bud." The guy lifted his head off the counter as if having been awakened by our conversation. "Let's doer again."

"Show me the money, Carl."

Carl turned his attention to me, maybe hoping I'd offer to buy him a drink.

I said to Bud, "I'm looking for a friend."

"Who isn't? Carl here is hoping one will come in." Bud chuckled. "Does this friend have a name?"

"Ken Liky."

He gave the name half a thought. "He doesn't come around here much anymore."

"Where's he living now?" I asked it casually, just between old friends.

"Same place as always, from what I've heard. But I haven't heard much."

"You don't mean he's still living at Cressie's old place?"

"As far as I know." Davenport was ten times bigger than Frytown, but the regular citizens of Candlelight were few. Bud leaned an elbow on the bar so we didn't have to speak so loud. He said, "Liky was doing pretty good for a while, I guess. Big guy, buying drinks. It was like the guy was celebrating his girlfriend's death instead of mourning it. Cressie was well-liked around here, you know?"

I glanced at the stool next to me. I did know.

"After a while," Bud went on, "I guess he got the hint and decided to take his luck and drinking elsewhere."

A customer came in. Bud picked up his rag and went down to where Carl sat. Carl jumped when given a slap on the shoulder. "Give Carl here one of your worst whiskeys, and I'll take a Bud, Bud." The customer laughed at his own joke.

The couple at the end of the bar laughed, too. The guy lifted his bottle in a salute as the woman slid off her stool and staggered my way toward the bathroom. She was somewhere north of fifty, skinny with eyes bulging out of a boney face. She smiled as she passed, her lips thin, one of her top teeth missing. From the boyfriend with her? Or was this a new boyfriend? Another bit of hope in the glass always empty?

Bud got the whiskey and beer for the customer and went down and refilled a new order for the couple before coming back to me. He said, as if our conversation hadn't been interrupted, "I just remembered. Liky was in here a few days ago, looking like he'd just run over his dog. He wasn't offering drinks, not even Carl. He didn't stay but a couple of minutes, that's why I didn't remember right off." He gave a nod down to where Carl was throwing the last of his drink to the back of his throat. "I heard him tell someone the devil was after him, but then, I don't figure you'd find God chasing his tail."

I took a drink of my soda. My mouth felt dry. *Maybe one. One couldn't hurt.*

One tequila, two tequila, three tequila, floor. Cressie's voice. It was what she'd half-sing to someone when they chided her for drinking a glass of club soda. I could almost hear her lilting laughter, the essence of congeniality she held for strangers and friends.

I put a five-dollar bill on the counter and got off the stool. "Good to see you again, Bud." I added another five to it. "And this here is for Carl."

"That's what I remember about you," Bud said.

Did he remember something about me? "What?"

"You never left without buying a drink for Carl or making sure someone was going to give him a lift home."

"Did I?" He was speaking of someone I had a blurred image of who I'd been, but this image I'd never clearly seen. Cressie, maybe, not me. Did he have us confused?"

I glanced down to Carl, who looked up with pleading, watery eyes. For a minute, it wasn't Carl I was seeing, but my father.

I got up and left.

"Hey, don't be a stranger," Bud called out. "If I see Liky, want me to tell him you're looking for him?"

I considered, then I decided there was no reason to explain that Kenny wouldn't be coming around anymore. "Sure," I said. "Tell him an old friend stopped by to say hello."

Before closing the door, I gave one last glance back to the stool where I'd been sitting. *See, no problem. You could probably come again if you wanted to.*

Then for a moment, I thought there was someone, sitting on my stool. At first, I thought it was the woman, having come back from the bathroom. Only, an angry shout punched the air, and I saw she was back on her own stool, leaning away from her boyfriend. She swung forward, putting both hands around his neck, her thin lips trying to quiet his.

I glanced again. There was something, faint...*like* someone sitting on the stool. And on Cressie's? Two figures, ghost movements of things past.

I'd blanked on the fact I wasn't driving the Mustang, and, at first, I couldn't find my car. Then just as I spotted Percy's pickup and headed over to it, I noticed a motorcycle parked several spaces back. Someone was sitting on the bike, helmet on. Even though I intently stared over at him, he didn't turn away. Was this the same biker guy from the hotel?

You're being ridiculous. There are lots of motorcycles.

That might be true. But it felt like motorcycles were circling me, moving in for the kill. I hurried to the truck, started the motor, and pulled out into traffic. I maneuvered around a couple of blocks trying to see if the guy on the bike was following me. When I got back onto East Locust, he'd disappeared.

I kept checking as I drove. I didn't catch sight of him, yet I headed toward I-74, moving beyond it and Hwy 6. I let a length of street come between me and where I'd been, before switching over to Middle Road. Checking and rechecking the review mirror, I pulled off onto Oakbrook Drive, a housing complex. I drove the entire cul-de-sac, driving slow, plenty of time as if I'd come to pay someone a visit and couldn't remember their house number. Having made the complete circle, returning back to Middle Road, I took a left, retracing the miles I'd driven, and made my way back onto East Locust, taking it until I came to Kirkwood, then east side Middle Road, following it all the way back and across to 16th Street. From 16th, I turned onto Grant.

The flat-faced shutterless house where Cressie rented a room stood on the corner of 16th and Grant. Her apartment had been on the second floor. Did Kenny still live here? I got out of the pickup and walked into the entry encountering a familiar faint funky aroma. I listened. Both apartments on the first floor offered no noise. I started up the stairs, wincing as the wooden steps creaked. At the top, I stopped and listened again before moving over to Cressie's apartment door. Making the same route I'd taken many times, I thought of it still as hers, as if when I knocked, she'd open it and let me in. I put my ear to the door. No sound. No one inside? I grasped the door handle. Of course, it was locked.

How much time did I have before Leveque notified the Davenport Police of Kenny's murder and asked to have his residence sealed and investigated? I knew the orders were in play as I stood in front of the apartment, still unsure why I'd come and why I didn't just let the police do their job. Did Leveque still have an APB out on me? Had he found out I was driving Percy's truck?

If I'd been thinking straight, I would have left at that moment, in complete gratitude, no one knew I'd been there. At least, they may not have connected me right away.

Eventually, they'd check the Candlelight, as I had, and if the bartender couldn't give them my name, he could identify my photo. The police would know I'd come back. They'd share that information with FPD, and Leveque would probably put a warrant out for my arrest. Why not? Wasn't I fleeing the scene?

But so far, I was beating the odds and the process. And this could be my one and only chance to figure out what Kenny had really been up to and why he'd been killed in my condo.

I knew I needed to search the apartment.

I moved around to the side of the building. A window on the second floor. It would open to the bedroom. Would it be locked, too? I didn't have time to find a ladder. Instead, I climbed a rose trellis, thorns and all, praying the webbed slates would hold me.

The window lock seemed to be old and broken. I tried to raise it, and it gave slightly, then stopped. I shoved again, and again, and it gave another inch. It took several tries and several inches before I got it open wide enough for me to skinny in.

A chubby doll dressed in a pink, glittery dress, holding a wand and wearing a crown, lay on the floor in the middle of the room. Her crown was crushed. Kenny had given the doll to Cressie after a huge fight. She was into everything Wizard of Oz.

The mattress was tipped against the bedsprings, sheets, and covers flung to the floor. Nothing remained on the top of the dresser as if someone swept it clean and emptied the drawers, their contents spilled out onto the clutter. Apparently, someone was looking for something here, too.

I left the bedroom and walked down the short hallway, past a small bath, to the living room. This room, too, looked as if a bomb had been set off. Since I had no idea what I was searching for, there was going to be no way to discover whether someone else hadn't found it.

Why was someone ransacking Kenny's place, and mine? Had they killed him after finding it?

Arms grabbed me. A pillow sack shoved over my head.

"Get her out of here," a man's voice ordered.

My first thought was that it was the police. They had arrived to the apartment before me and were waiting. But they wouldn't cover my head.

"Let me go." My arms were anchored to my sides by powerful arms. I could see a shadow of another person through the cloth. Male, but no facial features. No uniform that I could see. I began kicking toward the shadowed figure, arching back, trying to get the guy holding me to lose his grip.

Suddenly my arms were released, but just as suddenly, they were jerked hard. Restraints dug deep into my wrists. Not handcuffs. It felt like a thin strip of plastic.

"Shut her up." The voice across the room ordered. "I'll get the car."

I continued kicking. Struggling.

"Fuck!" One of my feet found the leg of the guy behind me.

"Try that again, and you're dead." Something cold and hard poked me in the back.

A gun? I stopped struggling.

"Look, I haven't seen you," I said, foolishly thinking I could talk my way out of the situation. "As far as I'm concerned, none of this happened."

A noise came from somewhere in the house. I screamed, "Help! Call the police!"

A dry, rough hand smelling of garlic and tobacco covered the sheet over my mouth. I gagged.

"Hold still!" The guy behind me ordered.

I kicked out and arched back.

Steps crossed the floor.

Running feet could be heard coming up the stairs.

The guy behind me called out as if surprised by who'd showed up. "What are you doing here?"

"Not part of the plan." The voice was low, menacing.

Hold it. Plan? From my viewpoint, it was a pretty sure bet if anyone was going to get hurt in this situation, it was me.

"Let me go!" I yelled.

"Doesn't look like you got such a bad deal out of this," the person holding me snarled.

"Party's not over, yet." Came the reply.

Then more steps on the stairs. "You going to take him, or do you want me to do it?" This voice asked.

The low voice lost its menace. "Nah, I got this."

"Come any closer, and she's dead." The voice behind me sounded suddenly nervous. A cool, point of steel met the skin at my temple. He yelled, "Elroy?"

"I think Elroy's taking a nap downstairs." The newest member answered.

The man's body stiffened. The gun pushed harder into my scalp. "I'll kill her."

Abruptly I was pulled backward. I struggled, throwing myself in the other direction. It caught the guy holding me off-guard. He weakened his grip. I threw my body weight toward the floor.

A gunshot.

I waited for the pain.

"Kelly, you got him?"

Someone kicked me as they jumped over me.

"Yeah, go. He's not going anywhere."

A door banged shut. Bedroom door?

It banged back open. "He's going out the back window."

Realizing I was still alive, I thought it best to offer help. "The window is broken. I barely shinnied my ass under it."

Another shot.

Okay, maybe my help wasn't exactly needed. I decided it was probably better to keep low. I pushed my face into the carpet, breathing in mold, dust, and probably five vacuum-less years.

Another shot. Further off.

"Got her." A new voice entered the room. I recognized it.

I was lifted up into a sitting position. The pillowcase was pulled off my head.

Leveque.

CHAPTER TWENTY-ONE

O utside, the street was full of police cars, and a bright, banana-yellow Corvette.

After convincing everyone I wasn't hurt, I stood next to Leveque by his car, watching as the DPD taped off their crime scene. Two uniformed officers escorted someone out the front door. He was wearing khaki trousers, a shirt, and handcuffs. He was tall, like the biker at the hotel, but while his body showed a membership at the health club, he did not carry the same girth. Then a gurney wheeled from around the side of the house. The person lying on it was shirtless and had a shoulder bandaged. A paramedic moved to the gurney's side, holding a saline bag. Two police officers followed. Once the stretcher was lifted into the back of the van, the doors closed, and an officer got into the front with the driver.

I had a bucketful of questions and began taking them out one at a time, tossing them at Leveque. "Who were those guys? How did you find me? I could have got killed."

"You might have if this guy here hadn't called ahead and let us know you were heading our way." The hotel elevator biker guy came up to Leveque and me.

"Hell of a thing, Snake. I wasn't sure whether you were going to shoot her or him." This came from the other biker, the one I spotted sitting outside the Candlelight.

"Agent Harley Thompson." He nodded over to the other biker, "Agent Oliver Kelly. He and I work undercover for the Iowa Department of Narcotics and Enforcement."

I glanced at Thompson's naked bicep where the cobra wound down his arm. He followed my gaze and laughed, "Nickname's Snake. But I assure you," he nodded to Agent Kelly, "we're the good guys."

Stupefied, I continued trying to ferret out what was going on. "You were following me," I said to Agent Kelly. "I saw you parked in front of the Candlelight."

Kelly nodded. "We thought you might stop by there. It was a guess. Thompson came directly here to Liky's place."

"Those two were here before me," Thompson said, meaning the two that had been apprehended. "I was just going to check them out when you drove up."

"I should quit working for the Feds and join the local police."

Leveque grinned. "This here is just one of my backup vehicles."

The three laughed.

"Hold it," I said to Thompson. "You almost got me killed." I turned to Leveque, "What are you doing here?"

Thompson said, "She always this hard to handle?"

"So far, she's been pretty easy," Leveque answered. "It can get a whole lot worse."

"Shut up, Leveque." I jumped at Thompson. "And you, you better have a good explanation for planting heroin on me."

"Heroin?" Both Thompson and Kelly exchanged quizzical expressions. "What heroin?"

"Pay Dirt. That's what it was, right? Heroin? Cocaine? Meth? One of those. You didn't think I'd find it and get rid of it before the State Trooper stopped me. But I did. I threw it out the window."

Thompson and Kelly again exchanged glances. Kelly muttered something to Thompson. Thompson took out his cell phone and moved off.

"Tell me about this State Trooper," Kelly said.

I was watching Thompson. He made a quick call, then punched in another number.

"He was a fake."

"How do you know?"

"The insignias on the shirt were that of a lieutenant. Lieutenants don't work patrol."

Thompson came back. "Okay, tell us exactly what happened after you left the hotel."

Evidently, I'd thrown them a curve. They didn't seem to know about the drugs or trooper. But if Thompson hadn't planted the baggie on me in the elevator, then who did?

I gave them the short version. "I found the Pay Dirt baggie when I was leaving the hotel." I eyed Thompson. "I thought you planted it on me when we were in the elevator." I checked for any sign that he might be lying because when he'd made the second call on his phone, he'd glanced slightly back as if to make sure he was far enough away so none of us could hear.

"Nope, not me," he said brusquely.

Kelly glanced at Thompson with a puzzled expression. Then he said to me, "Go on. Then what happened?"

"A trooper pulled me over. He ordered me out of the car so he could search it."

Again Thompson and Kelly shared private opinions.

Thompson addressed Leveque. "Detective Leveque, our meeting just got pushed up. Let's go. Follow Kelly."

CHAPTER TWENTY-TWO   WHY YOU?

OCTOBER 31ST, FRIDAY, LATE AFTERNOON

"Where are we going? What meeting? What are you doing in Davenport?"

We sat and waited until Agent Kelly came around with his bike. Then we followed him out of the neighborhood.

Leveque scowled, saying shortly. "Now's a good time to tell me everything you know."

"I've got nothing to say. I didn't do anything."

He stopped at a red light. He watched cross traffic while I steeled him with a scathing eyeful. I considered opening the door and getting out. Could either of them outrun me? Probably. Besides, where would I go? And if Leveque was going to arrest me, wouldn't he have done it by now? Although, he had no jurisdiction in Davenport. The Davenport Police would have to make the arrest. Yet, there were DPD officers at the apartment. None of them had paid attention to me.

When the light turned green, Leveque said, "Detective Sorensen at the PDP asked about you."

Okay, I was going to be arrested. I sucked in a breath. Kenny went to the police with his blackmail after all. I played dumb. "What did he want to know about me?"

"If you were still alive."

CHAPTER TWENTY-THREE

The thick smell of old popcorn mixed with body odor and stale beer rankled my nerves when Leveque led me into the Steer Rider Taproom. Like all bars, the light was dim. To the left, pool tables stood with lamps hung low over worn, green felt. Pool cues lay as if haphazardly tossed, and colorful balls held fixed positions. A game had been interrupted. To the right was a bar. A large framed picture of a rodeo contestant riding a bull hung above the bar mirror. Next to it was what I took to be the prize-winning belt. This tavern catered to the cowboy, shit-kicking types. Bikers wouldn't be welcomed.

A uniformed officer stirred next to me, quiet as a ghost.

Kelly stood across the bar along with Agent Thompson and two others dressed in suits. One of the suits had his back toward us. Kelly must have told him we'd come in because he turned around, and when he did, I recognized him. He was the man I'd seen sitting on Peggie's desk listening to Mayor Otis.

He broke away from the others and came over, his hand extended. "Detective Leveque. Good to finally meet you in person. You know everyone here, I believe."

Leveque took his hand and nodded to the suit sitting at the bar. "Commander Park and I met earlier today."

I understood then that the second suit must be DPD Commander Park.

The man I'd seen in Charles's office flipped open his shield and held it out to me. "Agent Samuel Stone of the FBI." He snapped it closed just as fast. "And you must be Lillian Dove."

I nodded. This was big brass. What did they want with me? Arresting me for breaking and entering, or killing Kenny wasn't a federal offense.

"Come on over and join us for a drink," he offered. "I'll fill you in. You must be curious why you're here."

No, not one bit curious. Totally terrified.

He led me beyond the bar to the back of the room, where small tables and booths offered private moments. Leveque stopped to speak with the Commander. Thompson joined us while Kelly stayed at the bar. It wasn't until I sat in one of the chairs that I saw two other uniformed officers in the dark corners of the room. We were heavily guarded.

I thought back to what the detective had asked Leveque--if I was still alive. Who was being protected in this room? Them? Or me? Again, why?

The Commander left without any further dialog with Agent Stone. Leveque joined us and took the chair next to mine. As soon as he did, the bartender miraculously appeared at our table and set in front of us three beers and a club soda with a slice of lime. Thompson and Stone each took a beer. Leveque stared at the last two drinks as if unsure which was meant for him. Then Stone nodded to the yet untouched club soda, and asked me, "Would you care for something else?"

The question came off as a taunt. For the first time, I took a moment to actually observe this man. He was older than Charles, and like Charles, he was seasoned. The seasoning showed in the small bags under his eyes from a lack of sleep, and the way those tired eyes gave me his full attention while still routinely checking peripherals. Although the room was heavily guarded, Federal Agent Stone was on edge.

I reached out for the glass, trying to stop my hand from trembling, not wanting him to think his ordering me a club soda rattled me.

Leveque took the last beer.

Few people were aware of my drinking past. I hadn't confided to Charles, although I'm sure he guessed. The first few dates when he'd ordered wine, I never drank mine. Eventually, he stopped ordering. Donna wasn't privileged to my story, either. While a friend, telling her might mean a public announcement. I'd confided in only one person, Amanda Keiff, the local librarian and the Baptist minister's wife. I can't say exactly why I came about making a confession to her. However, I offered only after she confessed to having an addiction to Danielle Steel romance novels. There's comfort in the presence of others that have accepted their flaws.

"I'm going to skip the preliminaries," Stone started, his drink remaining untouched.

"Please don't." I interrupted. "I want to know what's going on. Why do you think I'm involved? And I want to know if you're going to arrest me or not. If you are, then read me my rights so I can call my lawyer."

There was a round of chuckles. Stone smiled. "You're not under arrest. In fact, we hope you'll be willing to help us out."

"Doing what?" I think I may have preferred being arrested. It sounded safer.

"We've been working this case for over ten years, embedding our team into the My-erville Holdings Corporation." He paused as if waiting to see if I'd heard of the company. I shook my head. "It's a two hundred million dollar corporation based in Chicago taking steps to go public. It's primarily clean. That is, it appears clean."

Again, he paused as if what he said should have jogged my memory. "Axel Cole is the sole owner. He's set to financially make a bundle once the company goes public. The regulatory process for setting up a company on the stock exchange is more ruthless and intrusive than examining the next president of the United States."

He waited. Maybe he was waiting for a response to his joke. Not getting one, he went on. "The ATF got involved when Cole moved a small, illegal part of his original business into Davenport. It'd already been under suspicion of money laundering. Small com-panies. Mostly laundromats, small retail, and fast-food restaurants. The move triggered connections Cole had with the Chicago family."

Leveque broke in. "I still don't understand why he didn't just let that part of his history go after Myerville became so successful?"

"I thought your Dad gave you the story?" Stone said.

Leveque's face reddened with the reference. He took a swig of his beer. Then replied, a bit snidely. "I called him to check you out, not to find out more about the operation."

I twisted around to Leveque. His dad? Did he call his father to check out Agent Stone? FBI?

"Then he must have given me a thumb's up. You're here." Stone laughed. "Your old man and I go back a way. He said I'd never get you to agree to become involved." He gave another chuckle, seeing, like I saw, Leveque's expression sour. "He said you were done with the agency. Yet, I say again, you're here." Stone lifted an eyebrow, and chuckled again. "It gets in the blood, doesn't it?"

Leveque ignored the question.

Donna once told me she'd checked into Leveque when he first came on the force. She said from what she could find out, he came from the Leveques of New York. She said the name as if they were the Rockefellers. But she said nothing about his dad's connection to the FBI, or his. Had Donna missed something? It didn't seem possible. But if Leveque's father was high enough in the FBI that Agent Stone called him for information, just who was his father, and why was Leveque working in Frytown?

Leveque took another swig of beer, wiping the foam away from his lips with his hand. He set the bottle down on the table slightly harder than necessary. "I haven't said I was going to get involved. The only reason I'm here today is because of a dead guy in our morgue."

"You're involved whether you want to be or not, because she is," Stone said pointedly.

Okay, had they missed seeing I was sitting at the table? "I'm not involved."

Stone didn't seem to hear me. He continued on as if now he were speaking only to Leveque. "Cole's made a deal with the cartel, and he's hired companies to make the shipments. He got his start working the drug market with the family. He expanded, needing to redirect the monies made from it and the casinos he was handling. As you know, one of those companies that were laundering for him is located in your jurisdiction.

"Chicago's not happy with Cole's business dealings with the cartel, but they aren't stopping him. Cole broke away from Chicago twenty years ago. Invested illegal money into real estate. It's how Myer Development got its beginnings. He learned he was a pretty good businessman. Illegal monies became overlayed with legit wealth. Cole's going public because he has a son he's grooming and investing in politics."

"Can he do that?" I guess I was naïve.

Everyone at the table laughed.

"It won't be the first public company with a spider's web hooked to Wall Street." Stone nodded to Thompson. "Why don't you take it from here?"

I took the break in the narrative to whisper to Leveque, "Is your dad really with the FBI?" He ignored my question, his face stern, cheeks slightly sucked in.

Thompson said, "This is where you come in." But he wasn't talking to Leveque. All eyes were on me. "You're involved because Liky was indebted to Cole for drugs and gambling. Liky got word of Cole's financial expansion. Maybe Cole directly told him. For a time, Liky was pretty close to Cole's illegal deals. Doesn't matter how he came about knowing Cole was going to pull out of the family connections and illegal trade. But knowing it caused him to make a stupid decision. One that got him killed. He decided to try to take over some of the business Cole was leaving behind. Stupid move. If he would have kept his head down until the company went public, eventually, Cole may have forgotten him and anything Liky owed or was handling, ignored."

He said to Leveque, "Liky was only a small pimple on Cole's butt. Only, Liky got greedy and wanted a bigger corner of the drug market. Cole put a hit out on him."

Stone interrupted. "That's when everything became a bit more interesting. Of course, we'd been watching all of this from the sidelines, waiting to see where it was going and if an opening would show itself for us to stop Cole. Not only did we want to pin drug and money laundering charges on him, he was also involved in at least fourteen murders. That we are aware of. Only, Cole's a delegator. So far, we could never fully hold him."

"The hit was the beginning of this investigation. Well," Thompson said, "not the hit itself. Cole retracted the hit. Our sources began telling us that Liky got ahold of something. Something that could connect Cole to murder and stop his financial strategy. Knock his kid from any political bid, too."

Stone took back over. "We discovered Liky was blackmailing Cole. Liky wasn't just an avenue to getting Cole, he became our puppet. He already had a police record. With his hands digging deeper, trying to take over Cole's old business, we'd gathered enough evidence on him to put him away for a long time. So," Stone smiled big, "we offered him a deal he couldn't refuse. If he gave us what he had on Cole, we'd make sure he landed in a prison where a guy like him might survive." Cole leaned over slightly as if his joke needed to be further explained. "Liky was still young and a good-looking guy, if you know what I mean."

I offered a slight smile. I'd got the insinuation, no explanation needed.

Thompson picked up. "Liky came to understand he was either going to prison by the agency's accommodations, or he was going to end up like he did, with a bullet in the back of the head." Thompson shrugged. "He was a gambler to the end."

"Liky took off. We thought he was heading for Mexico or Canada." The voice came from behind me. Agent Kelly had come up quietly while Stone and Thompson had been talking. "Or Cole called his bet and buried him."

Thompson said, "Then Liky came alive, but he wasn't making contact with either Cole's people or ours. He led us to you."

I glanced at Leveque. This was a lot to take in. Besides, casting Kenny into a starring role seemed far-fetched. He never came across to me as being very smart. Not smart enough to pull off a con against someone like Cole, or outmaneuver the police.

How much of what they had been telling me had Leveque already known? Did he also know I was being followed by federal agents?

"Cole had your store tossed and roughed up your employee," Thompson explained. "When he didn't find what he was looking for, he headed over to your place. Liky had followed you back to Frytown. Broke into your place. He was cornered. Stupid fool." He added, "The first rule of business, don't shit in your own backyard."

No one spoke for a few minutes. Stone asked, "Lillian, where's the flash drive Liky gave you?"

"It's in my backpack in my car." Is that what they wanted? They could have it. "But I dropped it in a glass of water at the restaurant. Kenny was also trying to con and blackmail me."

"We know." He didn't add how he knew. "We also know you went back and got the drive."

The statement stunned me. How did they know? Had they been following me even then? Thompson, I'd seen in the hotel, not the restaurant. I would have considered his being at both more than a coincidence. Bald, wearing black leather, a tattoo of a snake. Not the type of man, when drinking or not, I preferred attracting.

I explained. "I went back to get it, wanting to see what he'd faked. He said he had proof I killed my friend Cressie." I turned to Leveque. "It was a lie. She committed suicide. Whatever he had on the flash drive, he'd created. I hoped an expert would be able to tell the difference."

I turned to each of the others in turn, just in case they thought anything they'd found out about Liky's connections to me might be true or connected to what he was up to. "The drive's water-damaged. Or there was nothing on it to begin with."

Stone said to Leveque. "You found the drive?"

Leveque gave a nod. "We had it checked. There was nothing on it."

Stone resumed. "Like we thought. I think Liky was bringing you something else, but you left before he could give it to you or plant it. It's why he followed you to Frytown."

I remembered what Kenny had told me. "He said he had the original memory card."

"He offered to give it to you?"

"If I bought in and accepted his con. Money, of course."

Thompson said, his voice low and serious. "He'd need to get further than Canada or Mexico to lose Cole. Cole would hunt him down to hell and back."

Stone asked Leveque. "Did your men find a memory card when they searched her place?"

Leveque made no answer. He pushed back his chair and got up, pulling his phone out of his pocket. He walked away while making the call.

"Kenny wouldn't have been coming to bring me the memory card," I said. "There'd be no reason for him to. I made it clear to him that he wasn't going to bluff me. Besides, I'm broke."

"I don't think Liky was bringing it to you to continue a con. You were still the perfect person to stash the memory card with. You weren't connected to him except by his girlfriend, who died five years ago."

Stone looked off over to Leveque. "We've tied together a few more pieces to the puzzle since Liky's unfortunate decision to try to play us and Cole both. We know what's on the card." He turned to me. "Your friend didn't commit suicide. Cole had her killed. In fact, we're pretty sure now he took personal charge in making sure her death was handled correctly. Unlike him. He hadn't dirtied his hands in years. But a bug like Liky? Blackmailing him? He took that personally."

What he said didn't make sense. The police reported Cressie's death as an alcohol-drug overdose. If her death was suspicious, the coroner would have investigated. Only, maybe someone like her, with a past, and alcohol and drugs on the premises, wouldn't motivate a coroner's office to perform an autopsy. There were budgets to consider.

I'm so sorry, Cressie.

Leveque came back to the table. "I've ordered her place to be given another search."

Stone glanced at his watch. "I've got to go." He ordered all three. "Find that memory card before Cole does."

"Why her?" Leveque stopped Stone.

"Yeah, why me?" A question I'd been asking since Kenny first came back into my life. "Can I go now? I don't have the card."

"Cole thinks she has it," Stone replied.

"Hold it." Leveque moved toward Stone.

Kelly cut in, stopping him midstride. "Too late. By now, Cole knows she's been talking to us. Commander Park said lawyers for the two we arrested arrived at the station and hospital before the dust settled. Cole thinks she's cutting a deal."

"He thinks she's cutting a deal?" Leveque challenged. "Or you've put it out there that she has?" He came back over to me. "Come on, Lillian. We're leaving." He pulled my arm, wanting me to get up, while saying to Stone, "Either way, if she cooperates or not, you're as good as putting a bullet in her head."

Hello boys, I thought. I'm right here.

"Sit down, Leveque," Stone ordered.

"Go to hell." Leveque spat.

"I said, sit down."

I sat. Leveque remained standing.

"She'll be safe. Kelly and Thompson, and you will be watching her twenty-four seven." The tone was official, almost threatening. "Chief Kaefring said I'd have the FPD's full cooperation."

Hold it. Charles knew about all of this?

Stone got up from the table, turning to Thompson. "Fill Leveque in on the schedule. I have an appointment to keep." He addressed Leveque one last time. "Sherman said there'd only be one reason you'd agree to work with us."

Leveque spat back. "Chief Kaefring doesn't know you're planning to drag her further into this. He'd never go for it."

"One way," Stone repeated. "Your father said I'd need to show you it was the only way to keep her alive. He said you're the Samson-type." He guffawed. "Watch those haircuts, Leveque, or you'll end up like Thompson."

Thompson gave a belly laugh and wiped his hand across his bald head. But as Stone walked away, his hand came back to the table, and his laughter cooled, his expression dissolving any humor.

I couldn't swallow, let alone speak. They were tossing me back and forth like a game of pitch. Stone, Leveque, and Cole. And Charles. It was plain now that he was a part of this game, too. Leveque wouldn't bother with me if not.

My only absolute conclusion to everything being said was that I was all on my own. I have an addiction to living. And I wasn't about to let anyone make decisions on my behalf.

CHAPTER TWENTY-FOUR

Thompson immediately started in as soon as Stone left the bar. "Dyre Moving is hauling product to Laredo, Texas, then taking it across the International Bridge into Mexico."

Dyre?

"All product is scheduled to leave Saturday night, midnight. We have agents watching all the other trucking companies. They're strung out in small towns like yours across Iowa and Illinois."

Kelly broke in, speaking offhandedly. "A little over twenty-four hours. Cole must be madder'n hell. Sure glad I'm not the sap who knocked Liky off without finding that chip first." No one at the table made a reply. The bar was eerily quiet, and while he spoke moderately, his words resonated. He grasped his beer and his fingers played with the label as he continued to think aloud. "Liky one-upped the agency. Swindler out-swindles the Feds. That's not a good headline if discovered. Stone's butt is on the line." He lifted the bottle, took a long swallow, then set the bottle down hard.

The hit blasted the quiet of the bar causing me to jump. Leveque's head snapped to Kelly.

Kelly said, "Whoever put that bullet in Liky's head before finding the memory card is a dead man walking." He brought his beer up again, paused, added, "That is if he's not already fish bait." He took another long swallow, then stood up. "Got to see a man about a horse." He got up from the table and headed back toward the restrooms.

Thompson, scowling, watched him go. There seemed to be a competition between the two. Or was Kelly alluding to something Leveque and I didn't understand? An inside joke?

"Cole's moving product if the drive's found or not." Thompson stretched out his index finger "This guy of yours, Pane, set Cole up with the shipping company in Frytown."

Pane? Our Councilman Pane?

He held out his middle finger. "Pane's a link Cole can deal with without being stung. The connection travels back to Chicago, money laundering, and then gets lost." His ring finger came last. No ring. No white line. "If we don't find that card or find a way to connect Cole to the shipments, then we're all fucked."

Kelly came back, addressing Thompson, "You ready?".

Thompson glanced at me. His tone again sounded like a threat. "Cole won't leave a loose thread."

I gulped. I wasn't so thrilled about being on someone's string.

Leveque stood. "Come on Lillian." He pushed past Kelly and started away. I saw no other choice but to get up and follow.

"You'll be hearing from us," Thompson called out before the barroom door closed.

CHAPTER TWENTY-FIVE

I started throwing questions as soon as we were back in Leveque's car, but he dodged them, chewing on his cheek, hands on the steering wheel, hard as fists. He wove the car in and out of traffic, almost sideswiping a car, before making an illegal U-turn and heading back the way we'd come. Kelly and Thompson were coming out of the bar as Leveque sped past.

"Slow down," I shouted. Stone was wrong. Cole wasn't going to kill me. Leveque was going to kill both of us.

A traffic light turned yellow. He stomped on the brake. The car behind squealed to a stop.

"The agency doesn't spin its wheels," he seethed, angry. "Stone wants what Liky had as badly as Cole does. It's my bet Chicago doesn't know about the drive, or if they do, they're interested, too. Everyone's watching you." He glanced over, eyes narrowing. "Get it? Stone doesn't give a rat's ass what happens to you. He wants the case win."

He continued staring at me as if I was supposed to respond. I didn't know much about law enforcement, but I guessed FBI outweighed a small-town police chief. "Maybe if you called your father, he could…"

It must not have been the response he was waiting for. His eyes ignited. He didn't wait for the signal to turn green. He tramped hard on the gas pedal. Mach one, faster than the sound of me screaming for him to stop and let me out.

More lights came up yellow. I continued to scream as he drove through them all.

They say right before you die, you see your whole life flash before you. I didn't see my life in its entirety. But I got a good view the last few hours, and what I saw was that Leveque wasn't so innocent. I suddenly realized, he'd been tossing me around as much as all the others. In fact, he may have been the one to make the first pitch.

That realization kindled a fire under me. "You played me?" I was no longer worrying about him getting us killed in traffic. He'd thrown me to the wolves at the very beginning. "You made it appear like I'd killed Kenny."

"Don't be stupid. You don't have what it takes to kill someone," he returned. "No one believed it."

"I do, too, have what it takes." Hold it. What was I saying? What was he saying? "Clarence's gun?"

The car slowed slightly. His tone was mocking. "I didn't say you killed him. I asked you where the gun was."

The pieces were there. Why couldn't I match them up? "I saw Stone at the station when I left. He was in Charles's office."

Leveque's jaw locked.

Then it was true. He and Charles were working with Stone even then. Had Stone watched while Leveque interrogated me? Was Leveque trying to gain points with Stone?

If Leveque had been with the agency, maybe he'd been fired. Why else would he have come to work for a small-town police department? He was using me to make points.

I began to pant from all the anger coursing through me. I needed to vent. Nothing I could say would stop them. Nothing that I could do would take back all Kenny, Leveque, and Charles had done to put me smack in the middle.

I realized if I was going to get out of all this, I was going to have to do it. That acknowledgment infuriated me beyond mere anger. How dare they!

I punched Leveque hard on the shoulder.

The blow caused him to lose control of the car. The car swerved. Horns began blaring.

I punched again.

"Stop it."

And again. I couldn't stop.

Horns honked. Brakes squealed. Tires skidded. Then there was the sound of a large crash.

"Are you crazy? Knock it off." Leveque made a sharp turn.

I continued to strike out, enraged, willing to do battle for what was mine.

He turned another corner, so sharply that my head snapped back, hard. Still, I came back swinging. It was my life they were all playing with. Not theirs, mine.

I punched him on the head, neck, and shoulder. I was so furious, I wasn't paying attention to my aim.

He braked to a stop. Grabbed and clenched my hands. "Stop hitting me," he yelled.

"You set me up," I yelled back. "You and Charles. I am lucky to still be alive."

"If you wouldn't have plowed ahead as you did with the arson fire last summer. I told you then to stay out of it."

You'd think what he said would have put spit on my fuming fire of outrage. Stay out of it? I'd have gladly stayed out of this if I hadn't been dragged in by Liky and now the FPD. Besides, I recoiled, "You had no idea who was involved in that arson until I told you."

His grip on my wrists grew tighter. He changed tactics. "If I hadn't shown up in Davenport, they may have arrested you for breaking into Liky's place. That could have linked you to his murder."

"They weren't going to arrest me," I returned. "They were all hoping I'd lead them to Cole. They were all using me."

I jerked to lessen his hold on my wrists. "I had no other choice but to show up. I wasn't fooled enough to think you were going to figure out who killed Kenny." I jerked again, struggling against his strength. Together, we were putting off so much heat, the windows began to fog.

Leveque didn't answer. But he did let go of my hands. "You're wrong. I didn't drag you into this. Liky did. You should choose your friends better."

Again, fuel added to flames. "If you knew so much, how'd my store get broken into? Percy hurt? From what they told me back there, the Fed's stopped it. Where were you?"

No comeback. He stared off beyond me.

Yet, something about the timing of the two events didn't add up. "But they weren't worried about me, then," I said, thinking as I spoke. "They thought they scared me off by planting the heroin."

"Huh?"

"The heroin," I told him, going over it aloud. Not for his benefit, for mine. The pieces were coming together. "I don't think Kenny planted the drug on me."

"So? Who then?" His voice was curious.

"If they'd all been watching Kenny, the Feds, and Cole knew I'd ruined the drive. So why would they have followed him to Frytown? The Feds could have just as easily asked the FPD to keep an eye on me. Unless they already knew about the memory card."

Come on, I willed myself. I knew I was getting close to figuring something important out. "They never cared about the flash drive. Kenny was blackmailing both Cole and the

Feds." While the last few hours were beginning to replay themselves in my head, there were still too many holes. "But why didn't they grab him, then, at the restaurant?"

"They weren't sure?" Leveque asked. "Maybe they didn't know about the card then."

Suddenly I realized Leveque was listening. The muscles in his face had relaxed as if his brain was mulling over what I was offering and comparing it to what he knew.

He shook his head. "Doesn't matter. Knowing any of this won't solve your problem now. You are in the middle of all this. A problem I don't need."

"Look, Samson."

His eyes ignited hearing Stone's tease again. He flushed.

"I don't need your help," I stated flatly.

"Honey, you're the bait. Don't you get it? Agent Kelly was following you. He was there the night your store was broken into. He saved Percy's life. But it could just as well have been you."

A question suddenly came to me. "Hold it. Why didn't they already know Kenny was dead? You reported it, right?"

"What?" From his expression, I knew I'd come up with a question he hadn't yet asked himself.

"If everyone had been surveilling Kenny, and Thompson and Kelly knew everything that was going on, then why didn't they already know Kenny'd been killed? Who knew Kenny was at my condo?"

Mixing pieces, the picture is fuzzy, but clearing. "Kelly stopped the car dragging Percy. Where was Thompson?"

He stared, his mouth hanging slightly open. He'd never admit it, but I'd asked a pretty interesting question. Seemingly one he couldn't answer.

He put the car back into gear. Took the first corner and then the next. Back on Locust, I glanced at where the crash happened. Lights flashed. A crowd had gathered. Two cars were stopped in the middle of the street. No police are at the scene, yet. If someone was blaming a crazed driver in a yellow banana Corvette, no one seemed to be out looking.

Turning onto 16th, he pulled the Corvette up next to Percy's truck. The muscles in his neck twitched. When he spoke, his voice was low, almost a growl. But this time, his anger wasn't directed at me. He sounded angry at himself. "Keep out of this, Lillian."

His cell phone rang. "Leveque here." He listened. "What do you mean she's moved back in?" He glared at me. "Did you tell her she could be arrested for breaking a crime seal? Then have Miner put her under arrest."

I wish I'd been playing the million-dollar question. I'd be rich.

He listened. "She what? Have you told the Chief this?"

He got off his phone. "Do you know what your mother's done?"

A hard question, but if he'd given me two, maybe three tries, I could have come up with a feasible answer. He didn't wait. "Miner went back to do a second search. He found her moved back in. She had the place cleaned."

Yep. I may have eventually come up with that answer if given time. "She can be pretty stubborn."

"Don't be stupid," Leveque barked. "She could have thrown away evidence we didn't find yet."

I only heard the word, stupid. A word Dahlia always used.

I hated that word.

I got out of the car.

Leveque got out on his side, ordering me like one of his officers. "You get your mother out of that condo. And don't do anything stupid until this is all over."

"Don't worry, Samson." I seethed. "I'm not planning to do anything, stupid. But my mother? You deal with her. She's not my responsibility anymore."

CHAPTER TWENTY-SIX   TRICK OR TREATS?

HALLOWEEN NIGHT

T he sun had set by the time I turned onto the I-80 back to Frytown. I didn't catch sight of Leveque following me, but I assumed he was keeping close tabs. I stopped for gas and grabbed some chips and a Pepsi. I was starved.

Exiting Hwy 218, I circled off, passing the Gas for Less, open and busy. I wondered if Percy was feeling better. Passing the police station, all seemed quiet. Neither Charles's cruiser nor his Ford Explorer was in the parking lot. If it was, I'd have stopped and given him an earful. Maybe a punch or two, too. I wanted to know when he met Stone. Why did he let Leveque interrogate me? Although, if Stone was listening in, it explained, now, why he let Leveque go on as he did.

Stone had investigated me beyond my living in Frytown. That was clear by his ordering the club soda. Ordering the drink was his way of showing me he was in control of the situation.

Well, I was taking back control.

As I continued into town, I realized I'd forgotten it was Halloween night. Pumpkins were lit, graveyards taunted, and house lights flickered. Recorded shrieks and screams added to the weird vibe. The atmosphere was a little unnerving after all that had taken place in Davenport.

Costumed trick-n-treaters, carrying heavy bags of candy, maneuvered up and down the sidewalks. These were mostly older kids, and teenagers. Some wearing their cheerleader outfits for costumes.

Coming to Lincoln Avenue, a witch with a black hat and two football players were walking away from Donna's house. The three stopped, glanced into their bags, and started laughing. What was Donna handing out? Ginger Snaps?

The front of her house was well lit, and a couple of cars were parked in her driveway. It's then I remembered she was having a Bobby Bowen party. The mayor's alleged illegitimate wife was on the show. Would Bowen produce a marriage certificate with the mayor's name on it? Was the mayor really a bigamist?

I would never have bet on it. But I also would never have bet Morton Dyer could be involved with someone like Axel Cole. Did Dyer know his customer and what product he was shipping?

Stone said something about how Councilman Pane put Cole and Dyer together. How did Stone put it, payback for an earlier time?

I slowed again at Harding Avenue, where a patrol car blocked the street. Next to it was Charles's cruiser.

The mayor's Victorian residence, once belonging to a founding father, seemed to have every light blazing. The street was crowded with news vans. Uniformed officers stood on the lawn, trying to control both the gawkers and the news media. I saw Councilman Pane's Cadillac parked in the mayor's driveway.

If Councilman Pane was involved with someone like Axel Cole, was the mayor also involved?

Again, I was tempted to stop and give Charles a piece of my mind. But, I was exhausted. My wick was burning down.

I turned off the main track and traveled past Discount. I saw the seal on the door. A crime scene. Won't that be good for business?

I came to where I would normally turn to go to Lake View and the condo. But, I couldn't go there.

Get your mother out.

Dahlia made her own bed, she could lie in it. She could deal with the police. Maybe they'd arrest her. Wouldn't that just tickle *me* pink?

CHAPTER TWENTY-SEVEN   RUN FOR COVER?!!

MIDNIGHT

I drove on to Church Street, to the small house with black numbers, 772. This time, I didn't stop in the driveway. I got out of Percy's truck, unlocked the front door, and went quickly in. Going over to one of the windows, I pulled back the curtain and checked out front. I was almost sure Leveque followed me. But I wasn't seeing him.

"Don't do something stupid."

How dare he!

Dim yellow light from street lamps spotted down onto the sidewalk. House lights had been turned off, pumpkin candles blown out, and trick-n-treaters moved on to a more affluent neighborhood or tucked into bed.

I stood staring into the dark, wanting to blame Charles for not believing in me enough to confide what was going on with Agent Stone. I was furious at Leveque for not following me and making sure I was safe like he said he would.

Most of all, I was mad at everyone for thinking they could play me like a fool.

I am nobody's fool.

I turned away from the window. This was only the second time I'd been in Clarence's house. The first time was when his estate lawyer handed over the keys. Then, I made a quick tour of the place and left. Even though it was my house, I felt like a complete stranger.

I still did.

The only light coming into the room was the hazy, ghostly yellow from the street lamps. I stood in the middle of the room, smelling a whiff of his pipe tobacco. He was still here. Do we ever really leave? He was so present in the house that it felt like if I said his name, he would answer back.

The room contained a couple of club chairs, a hassock, small lamp tables, and a coffee table holding a large Mexican sombrero ashtray with his pipe and tobacco pouch set alongside. A flat-screen TV hung like a framed painting between a set of windows facing the front. A bookcase overfilled with paperbacks stood on one wall, and a small curio cabinet stood across from it, holding the space between the two front windows.

The curio cabinet was of the type someone might keep framed family photographs. There were no pictures. Instead, the cabinet held souvenirs from vacations he'd taken. He'd told me one of his goals had been to visit every state in the United States, but he never made it past Oklahoma. "Couldn't find anyone I could trust to take care of the store. You can't leave a business unattended."

His voice. I could hear it as clearly as if he was in the room with me. "Can't leave a business unattended. Won't last long if you do." What would he say now, knowing because of me, there may be no more business?

Don't go there. Everything will be fine, my old friend whispered.

One thing about denial and negating truth, if not totally understood, it can also sound like hope. It's perspective, I guess.

Exhausted, I traveled around making sure everything was locked up tight. The front door held a deadbolt, and the back door was secured with a chain and deadbolt. Clarence believed in security. From what? Most folks in Frytown leave their front doors unlocked. He also had a gun in the store. Did he really think he'd be robbed?

Although, come to think of it, Percy was attacked. I guess anything can happen, no matter who or where you live.

After seeing I was locked in safe for the night, I went into the kitchen. The refrigerator was empty. The cupboards bare. My stomach growled. I hadn't eaten and was starved.

But I was also dead tired. Food wasn't my first priority.

The door to the first bedroom stood open. An oval braided rug covered most of the wooden floor. Inside was a small bed, dresser, and a chair for sitting while putting on shoes. Someone who didn't know any better might think the room was for guests. Only, I'd been in this room before. I knew it was the room Clarence claimed as his. The walk-in closet held his clothes. The bureau contained his things. A Bible on top of the dresser had his name in it. A dedication from his mother. A gift.

The responsibility to pack his things and get rid of them was mine, but that would mean I'd have to decide what to do with the house. Move into it or sell?

My choices may have narrowed. I might have to sell the house to save the store.

Think of that tomorrow.

Right. I just wanted to crawl into bed and pretend today never happened.

Sleep.

I made my way to the second bedroom. Opened the door. This was the larger room of the two. It held a queen-size bed, a large dresser with several drawers, a mirror above a bureau, and a comfortable chair for reading late at night. The bed covering and curtains were a feminine soft yellow. A soft pastel green throw lay neatly arranged across the chair's arm, and pillows decoratively placed on the bed all led me to think a woman had a hand in putting this room together. I knew the closet in this room, as well as the drawers of the chest, were empty. For how long?

In all the years I'd known Clarence, he'd never mentioned a wife. Donna and I spoke of him many times, and she never mentioned a Mrs. Salzberg. Had she died? Is that why he carried a lonely demeanor even though he was liked by so many?

Is that why he left the house and store to me? Because he had no one else?

When I pulled back the bedspread to crawl into bed, strong feelings of sacrilege moved over me. If Clarence didn't sleep in this room, in this bed, how did I dare? But I wasn't comfortable sleeping in his bed, either.

There was little choice other than going back to the living room.

Positioning two of the club chairs at opposite ends of each other, I placed the hassock in between. When complete, even this makeshift divan beckoned a welcomed invitation.

I returned to Clarence's room and stripped his bed of the covering, taking one of his pillows. What was the difference in sleeping under his bedcover with my head on his pillow on a makeshift bed instead of crawling into his? Can't say. Sometimes reason doesn't play into decisions.

Taking off my jeans, I crawled under the cover. A stale aroma tickled my nose, dust from the house having been closed. The itch to sneeze took my mind back to lying on Cressie's living room floor, gunshots riveting above my head, men yelling, calling out commands, my life threatened, and breathing in the dust and ruin of what I have now learned were the lives of two people I intimately knew.

Cressie was my friend. I loved and missed her. Kenny? I never liked Kenny. But it was sad remembering him lying on my kitchen floor, solitary, forsaken. A life wasted. In some ways, he touched my life as resolutely, if not more so, than Cressie had. Because of her, I learned sobriety. Because of Kenny?

You didn't give in, Cressie. How could I ever have thought you had? I should have believed in you.

Agent Kelly claimed Cole killed her. Why? Especially when it was Kenny who owed him the money?

Why had Kenny decided to use me to save himself? Was I all he had left?

Am I to find reason in all of this?

I heard a noise. Something outside. I strained and listened. Or was it just my nerves? No one knew about this place. Well, that wasn't exactly true. All of Frytown knew I inherited the house, but they also probably knew I'd left it empty and never visited. Maybe it was Leveque.

I got up and looked out. The street appeared deserted.

What time was it? I found a small clock on one of the tables. It was going on midnight.

Another noise. This time it sounded like one of the other windows in the room rattling. I moved away from the one I was standing in front of. Was someone watching me? What if someone tried to break in? It's then I realized I hadn't anything to defend myself.

I thought of the gun Clarence kept at Discount. Was it the same gun that killed Kenny? If so, that meant whoever trashed Discount went there before going to the condo.

"You don't have what it takes to kill someone?"

Yeah, maybe Leveque was right. But I could hoot like hell, making whoever did break in think I could kill them.

I started checking in closets and drawers for another possible gun. If Clarence had one, he might have two. Especially since security seemed to be such a concern for him with the way he kept the house locked up so tight. Again, I wondered why, but decided coming out with answers that could never be answered wasn't a good use of time.

I watched the windows for movement as I moved from one room to the next. Finding only Clarence's cane to protect myself with, I then realized I didn't have a cell phone. If something happened, I couldn't call for help. That took me on a search for a phone. I found one in the kitchen, hanging on the wall, with a long, curled cord attached. It was an old princess line phone. Antique.

The line was dead. I flicked the light switch and found the lights turned off. Figured. I hadn't put any of the utilities in my name. Suddenly I didn't like staying in the house by myself.

I returned to the living room. Crawled back into my club- chair bed and pulled the covers over my head. Cole may have found out about my store. Kenny had, hadn't he? He may also have found out about the condo.

But, no one knew about Clarence's house.

I hoped.

CHAPTER TWENTY-EIGHT OR GET TO THE BOTTOM OF IT?
NOVEMBER 1ST, SATURDAY, AM

I awoke. Still alive. Freezing cold.

I got up and slid on my jeans. My stomach growled. I needed to eat. And I was still tired. Every creak and groan throughout the night had startled me awake. Maybe staying at Clarence's wasn't an option.

I opened the front door to go out to Percy's truck and found the Mustang parked in the driveway. Percy's truck was gone.

The car was unlocked. On the front seat set my cell phone. How did it get here? I picked it up and called Leveque. "My car's in Clarence's driveway."

"Who's this?"

"Who do you think it is?"

"I have a plan. We need to meet."

"Leveque. My cell phone wasn't in my car."

There was a paused silence. "It had to be. You must have dropped it. The techs found it inside."

He'd already heard about the State Trooper stopping me and searching for the planted heroin. I told him now about how the same said trooper pocketed my cell phone.

Leveque was quiet, then said, "Are you sure, or you just thought he did? Maybe he tossed it in the car."

I returned, "No. He took it with him."

"I'll think about that later," was his answer. "Can you meet at two? I should be ready by then."

"Ready for what?"

"You and the Chief like the Italian Kitchen on Lakeside, right? Let's meet there."

"Is Charles coming?" I'd feel better about going if Charles was going to be there, too.

He didn't answer. But I figured whatever plan Leveque had in the back of his tiny brain, he'd already coordinated it with Charles.

Ten o'clock. I had four hours to kill. Okay, wrong use of words. What plan had Leveque come up with? Was he putting me out for bait, like Stone? Would Charles agree to it?

I wasn't going to wait until two o'clock to find out. I punched in Charles's number.

"Frytown Police Department."

"Donna?"

"Lillian, where are you? Hold on." She took another call, and came back on the line. "Don't you worry about Percy. He's going to be just fine. He came by this morning to get his truck. Came in for a donut and a cup of coffee. Of course, he wanted to hear about the goings-on with the mayor."

She didn't take a breath. "You heard, didn't you? Jessica Feldman was on Bobby's show, and she does have a marriage license. Signed by the good ol'state of Iowa. Hold on." Another call. When she came back on the line this time, she jumped topics. "Melissa's out sick today, Hon, so I'm handling the phones for the first shift. Couldn't have been a worse time for her to get her period."

I tried to bring her back to where she left off. "Are you saying the mayor married this person before his wife died?"

Only Donna wasn't finished with her thought. "What's wrong with girls today? When I was Melissa's age, if I got my period, I thanked God, padded up, and went to work. No lying around rubbing my tummy and complaining about cramps. Sweetie, you're gonna have to hang on.

"Yep, Hon." She came on again, this time answering my question. "From the way it sounds, he married her two years before Corabelle found out she had cancer. I never would have believed it if I hadn't seen it with my own eyes." Of course, she hadn't seen it with her own eyes. She watched the Bobby Bowen show. But Donna never missed her weekly reality shows and would swear they were as real as her own life.

She said, "That was Doris Maxwell who called. She wanted someone to come over and check on a car outside her place. She said the guy had been sleeping out in it all night. Said he looked suspicious. I sent Cooney to check him out." A small squeal, "Ah oh, hang on." Again she picked up another call.

At that exact moment, patrol car twenty-six drove past. The lights weren't flashing, and the car was moving slowly. He passed Doris Maxwell's house, a couple of blocks down from Clarence's. I saw the car then, a dirty, old blue. The patrol car stopped and pulled to the curb. Cooney must have caught the license plate and called the number in because he seemed to be waiting to see if there were any outstanding warrants.

The patrol car pulled into a driveway. Pulled back out. Cooney was coming back.

"Donna, I've got to go."

"So do I, Hon. I'm busier than a mother cat with kittens. Everyone wants to talk to the chief. Newspeople have been outside since the mayor was arrested."

"He's been arrested?"

"He should have got worse than that. Cheating on Corabelle while she was having chemo. If I get close to him, I'll beat him alongside the head."

Cooney stopped in front of the blue car. He got out.

"Tell Charles I called, Donna. I need to talk to him as soon as possible."

"Will do. But don't expect him to call back anytime soon, Sweetie. Hey, before you go, how's your kitty doing?"

"Bacardi?"

"You found him, right? Over at your neighbors? A Mr. Earl Langley. Whoops, gotta go. I'll let the Chief know you called."

I got into the Mustang. I drove down the street. Passing the blue car, I saw who Cooney was talking to. Agent Thompson.

CHAPTER TWENTY-NINE

I tore off the crime seal and walked into Discount. If they hadn't arrested Dahlia, they weren't going to arrest me.

I'd swept Thursday night, and picked up smashed baggies of chips and nuts, but an eyeball accounting of the amount of broken glass compared to full bottles calculated that most of my inventory was gone.

I spent the next couple of hours sweeping, mopping, and checking what was salvageable. At first, I bent to the task with angry energy. Why me? But as I progressed, finding a great many of the expensive bottles still sellable, my mind also cleared.

It's going to be fine.

I could sell Clarence's house. I could start all over again. I could start now. New day. New life.

It'll be better tomorrow.

I continued to work, keeping my mind on the task. As I sorted and trashed, I found more good than bad. I found enough product to make my shelves appear full. There was a carton of Vodka I hadn't put up on the shelves yet. The beer in the cooler hadn't been touched. I spaced out the snacks on the rack. If you were new to the store, you might not notice. But, if you were a regular, you'd think the place was looking a little sparse. But, it's not like I was out to fool anyone. All of my customers knew what had happened here.

I went over to the cash drawer to count the money. Percy had been busy. I started him with two hundred. There were well over five-hundred dollars in the drawer.

So, the money hadn't been the motive? The flash drive?

Why would he think the flash drive was hidden here? My apartment would be more likely. Especially since I was coming home from Davenport, and the trooper searched the car. The likelihood of me having it was slim. Yet, whoever it was had still took the risk of coming to the store.

"What did the detective want to know about me?"

"If you were still alive."

Why would Cole want to kill me? Unless he thought I was in partnership with Kenny, and I would continue the blackmail.

I checked the space beneath the drawer where Clarence kept the gun. Gone. So, the person who damaged the store used the gun to kill Kenny. To implicate me?

"If you were still alive."

I closed the shop. My mind spun with everything that had happened. So much so, I weakened, getting no further than the steps. I sat down.

Why was my cell phone in the car? And who had put it there?

I pulled my cell phone out of my purse and started flipping through the apps. Could they have used my phone to follow me back to Frytown? Finding nothing, I got up and went over to the Mustang, I crawled on the ground, looking under the bumpers, and the carriage. What did a tracking device look like?

Unable to find anything that didn't appear applicable to the car, I returned to the steps.

I sat looking down the street where I knew Agent Kelly pulled in front of the car dragging the valiant Percy. He saved Percy's life. The big lug would have held on forever.

Did Kelly recognize one of Cole's men? If so, why didn't he think to go over to my condo?

And why was Agent Thompson sitting in a car down the block from Clarence's? In fact, how did he know about Clarence's house and that I'd be there? Did Leveque tell him?

From Leveque's attitude, I had the feeling he didn't like playing by the Fed's rules and wouldn't offer Thompson any information.

I pulled out my cell phone again, scrolled past the social media I rarely used, thumbed past the games I only played when bored, and I finally saw a green app with three white cookie-cutter people and the letters GPS imprinted over their heads. They'd put a tracker on my phone.

I checked the time. Close to one o'clock. Leveque wanted me to meet him in an hour. I had exactly sixty minutes to come up with my own game plan.

I deleted the app and turned off *location* on my phone. Getting back into the Mustang, I drove to Lake View. In the rearview mirror, I saw Thompson. He was keeping several blocks back but close enough to keep his eye on me.

If I had all these eyes, then surely I was safe.

They wanted me to be their pawn. Okay. So be it. But the next move was going to be mine.

The condo door was locked. I heard a crash. Someone was inside. I knocked. No answer. "Dahlia?" Donna said she'd moved in. Even the FPD couldn't stop her.

Each condo had a small patio. I'd had to scale the wall when someone broke into the condo last summer.

I left and hurried around the building. Was it Dahlia? Would they actually leave her there alone? Or was someone back searching again for the memory card?

I tackled rose bushes, toed the wall, and heaved myself up, gripping the wall's edge with my fingers. I was going to need to give up Pepsi and chips. Grappling to keep hold, I peered over through the sliding glass doors. I found Dahlia sitting in her wheelchair. She was making motions with her arms as if giving someone instructions. And there was something on her lap. Bacardi! The traitor!

Suddenly she turned. Saw me.

I fell. Hit the ground.

I screamed as someone grabbed me. My mouth and nose were immediately covered. I inhaled something sweet, antiseptic. My eyes started to close. Who was it? I squirreled around. What was it? I thought I saw or heard something I recognized, but I couldn't quite...everything went black.

CHAPTER THIRTY

Windshield wipers rake the snow off the windshield in shuddering rasps. I twist around and peek over the back seat. Frank and Patrick, wearing their PJs with the feet in them, are tucked under a blanket. Warm. Safe.

"Crazy havin' to take these babies out this time of night. In this cold," Dahlia snaps.

Babies. Younger than me.

Frank's eyes grow large. He stares at me, hard. He thinks it's my fault he'll have to go to bed when we get home. Not yet eight o'clock. When we do get home, *the shit'll hit the fan*. I mouth sorry, but he blinks and continues to hurl daggers.

"Lillian, turn around in that seat and sit down."

He'll pinch me when she's not looking. Pinch me hard. He hates me. Patrick will pinch me, too. He always copies Frank. They both hate me. They both think she's my fault.

You're like their little mama. Now, you watch them.

The heater's turned high. Mama's sitting straight, hands on the wheel, staring mean at the bad weather. *Colder than hell.* Daddy didn't make it home. *Now we've got to go get 'im.*

Like magic, out of the dark, the neon martini glass shines brightly. The celestial vessel empties and refills, body and blood of my father. It is here he comes in his sadness looking for solace. Looking for forgiveness. Love. Why doesn't he love me?

The glass is mesmerizing. Empty, full. Never empty. Never full. Sins of the father.

Your sins, too.

"Go on in and get 'im." We park opposite the door. She gives me a slight push. "Go on." The car door's heavy and clunks open, throwing me to the curb. "Shut that door before the heat gets out. Want these babies to catch a cold."

Icy wind slaps my face, snow heavies my eyelashes. The martini glass blinks on and off, flows full, runs empty. I trudge through snow higher than my galoshes, my toes beginning to freeze. I'm tired and hungry. I want to go to bed. I don't care if he doesn't get home. I don't care if he never comes home. I don't care if she never loves me.

The closer to the door I get the more I feel the tears welling, but I can't cry. It'll make her mad if I do.

Quit cryin' over spilled milk.

It'll make him sadder.

The heavy door to the bar opens lightly. The room's dark. The bar's nearly empty. Music plays in the background. Christmas songs. *Little Town of Bethlehem*. I hum along, eyeing each stool, looking for him before I move entirely in.

There he is. His head's lying on the bar, his face turned to the empty glass in his hand.

How still we see thee lie.

I yank on his coat. "Daddy?"

"Another one for the road?" The man behind the bar asks my father, bottle in his hand. He notices me. "Hi there..." He doesn't remember my name, but he knows me. He once said he knew me almost as well as he knew his own daughter. "Your mama outside?"

I nod and grab my dad's coat and give it another sharp tug. I don't like the man behind the bar. Daddy likes him more than us.

If I can't wake him, Mama'll have to get out in the cold and come in, and all hell will break loose where people can see.

The man wipes the scarred bar and a rancid stench rises stinging my nose.

Darkness. Drifting.

CHAPTER THIRTY-TWO

The warm air stings my cold face when I open the door. Christmas music plays quietly behind voices laughing.

"What can I get you tonight, Lillian?" Bud, behind the bar, stands before me as soon as I sit down on my stool. "Your usual?"

I am about to nod assent but change my mind. "Give me a martini. One like the sign outside, that never empties." I laugh. He laughs, too.

I've said it before. My joke.

I look at the stool next to mine. Empty. I feel lonely.

"Can do?" Bud offers a hollow grin, like a Halloween pumpkin, large and bright, masking the darkness within. His hands snatch up bottles, grab necks like hummingbirds' beaks, offering nectar to make *all merry and bright*. He shakes a tumbler, pours the drink into a martini glass and places it on a square, white napkin. Then he moves on to the next stool. "Your usual?"

Yet in thy dark streets shineth an everlasting light.

I twirl the glass, holding the magic in my fingers, and pray I can go this one night without taking a sip. The glass is mesmerizing. Empty, full. Never empty. Never full.

Who hears my prayers? Cressie's gone. I'm alone.

I raise the glass. Its slick texture wets my lips, slides icy on my throat, treating the pain, deadening the loss of love, the taste of bitterness: yellow bile of loathing for her, her hatred of me, my disappointing her. The glass empties and I replenish truths never true. Don't need her. Don't need anybody.

"Can't do it by yourself. Need to ask for help."

Miraculously Cressie is back. She sits on her stool holding a club soda with a twist of lime.

"You're alive!" I cry.

"As alive as you?" She laughs and lifts her glass. She takes a long, satisfying sip then glances down the bar. "I see the family's all here."

"I can't believe it's you." Is it really her, or did Bud put something in my martini? Is Cressie like one of those purple, polka-dotted elephants others joked about?

Yet, I see her clearly. So undoubtedly. Her long blonde hair flows to her waist. Her brown eyes snap with laughter. A scent she is wearing? Something different, but pleasing. She smells as fresh and new as a baby.

"You need to believe in something," she says.

The hopes and fears of all these years...

She reaches over and pulls the glass out of my hands.

I scream. "No. Cressie. Don't!"

She puts the drink to her lips. But the glass stays empty. Then, in her hands, it fills. She gives it over to me.

"If you can't believe, pretend to believe. Believe in me. Believe in her."

Help her.

"Who?"

"She's the key. Help her." She laughs.

"Who!"

"You silly."

The dark night wakes, the glory wakes.

Drifting. Dark.

CHAPTER THIRTY-THREE

"Lillian, shhh,"

I giggle. We're sneaking down the steps. I'm holding presents in my hands. It's Christmas. We left the stereo on. *Little Town of Bethlehem*. One of my favorites.

He is behind me. "Shhhh, you'll have them up."

But I can't wait for the morning. I can hardly believe everything I have ever wanted in life is right here, with them, with him. He pulls the hair from off my neck. Kisses me. "I love you." And before I can protest--that if *he* doesn't quit, he'll have the whole house wide-awake-- his lips move from my neck to my ear, the faintest of kisses, and I hear a deep moan of desire.

His? Mine?

My hands tremble. The presents drop heedlessly to the floor. I turn. I can't see his face. It's too dark. But when my lips seek and find his, yes, yes, with each kiss, it's him.

You've found the key, Lillian.

Yes, I hear myself answer. I found the key. It's always been mine to have.

He holds me back. "Where have you been?"

"Here, silly." I take his hands and pull him toward the Christmas tree. Presents no longer a priority. "Shhh..." I remind him. "Don't want to..."

He laughs, puts his finger to my lips.

We lay next to the Christmas tree, a scent so green and new. He kisses me leisurely, my eyes, nose. My hands bring him tight against me.

Slipping off my gown, his lips brush my breasts, then move lower to that part of me throbbing, pulsing, wanting him and...and...his mustache scratches, he's slobbering...he...he's too rough...Quit...Get off me!

CHAPTER THRITY-FOUR HIT BOTTOM

NOVEMBER 1ST, SATURDAY, SOMETIME AFTER 2 PM

I startled awake. My eyes worked to focus and distinguished a large black nose and a long red, wet tongue.

"He likes you." Someone laughed.

I screamed, tried to untangle myself from beneath long, muscular legs. My movement caused the Doberman Pincher to lick and pin me down all the more.

"Ramses, that's enough." Again laughter.

Who? Where?

The dog jumped off the couch.

My head whirled. My stomach upheaved as I struggled to my feet.

Ramses barked.

I sought protection and fled, stumbling around an armchair to use as a shield.

Where was I?

Ramses lopped behind, barking, excited. He leaped onto the chair, puffing the remnants of a dog bone, his tongue lolling out of his mouth, dripping wet. White sharp teeth. He barked. Bounded to lick me again.

"I suggest moving more slowly," the same voice said. "The drug you were given has, unfortunately, some lasting effects. It'll take a while to completely leave your system."

Hazily, I took in a good size room with a couch where I'd lain. A conversational area of chairs around a low table where a large gold cross set center on the glass top. A minister's home? Only this cross had four branch-like bars crossing the stake. Dimly lit by low lighting, paintings hung on walls. Again, at first, I thought of them as religious scenes, but then my mind noted Egyptian pyramids. The glass case next to a small cocktail bar held busts of ancient figures.

At the very far end of the room stood a desk, ornate and what appeared to be gold-leafing. Next to it, another bust. This one set atop a tall marble stand. The statue offered a black, stern face staring out beneath a gold cobra headdress. In front of a fireplace, a small but elegant table was set with plates, bowls, and glasses, and in the middle was a soup tureen, as if dinner was being offered inside due to the cold night.

"Allow me to introduce myself."

I whipped around, almost forgetting I was not alone. He'd moved. He'd placed himself between me and the only door. He was dressed in slacks, dress shirt with sleeves rolled and collar opened. Bushy eyebrows arched above deep, unsettling dark eyes. A well-manicured, grey mustache mounted full lips and then eased around into a goatee trimmed to outline his strong, firm jaw. He was not just good looking. He was statuesquely handsome. Intimidating. I knew his name before he said it.

"Axel Cole." He took a step toward me.

I stepped back. The Doberman whined from his chaired position.

"Ramses, let her get her legs under her." He grinned. "I think he's fallen in love."

"How did you?" My memory popped. I was at the condo, trying to get in. Someone was inside. I saw Dahlia. Then…then…?

"Doesn't really matter how? Does it? Let's just say I am very adept at getting my way." He grinned again, his lips pulling apart as if needing to breathe through his mouth, his eyes narrowing slightly. "Generally, my invitations to dinner aren't so brusque. But etiquette may have to be foregone in lieu of progress. You have become an obstacle to my success." His eyes narrowed to a slit. He swayed slightly. Then hissed, "An unsolicited hindrance."

His eyes opened and his tone brightened. "Come. Sit. It's a meager meal. The accommodations aren't my usual fare, but once you've had food, I am sure you'll feel better. And while we're eating, we can discuss how to mutually resolve our situation." He ordered, not with a loud or rough tone, but as a man who didn't need to raise his voice to get what he wanted. "Ramses, down."

"Where am I?" Was I still in Frytown? Or had I been taken somewhere nearby? Could I have been out long enough to have been transported back to Davenport?

Dreaming. I felt like I had come out of a long, long sleep.

Ramses obeyed the order, but he wasn't ready to give me up. He circled around the chair where I stood, forcing me backward further against the wall. He came straight to me and put his long, black nose to my crotch. Embarrassed. Feeling violated. I went to put my hands on his head to push him away. A menacing growl stopped me. He tucked his nose even tighter, and I swear, the dog inhaled.

Axel Cole guffawed. "You randy beast." He came around the chair. I wasn't sure if he was going to help free me or join in. I tensed. Ramses must have taken my movement as a sign of mutual desire. He wiggled his nose delightedly.

Cole barked with laughter.

His face drew close to mine. "Don't worry," he murmured, "I'm not going to let anything hurt you." He grabbed the dog by the collar, pulling him away. The Doberman didn't resist his nose being unplugged. He immediately sat on his haunches, his red tongue hanging, yet his beady black eyes held glued to my crotch. As if with the right word, he would gladly return.

"He seems to have taken an instant liking to you. Usually, he's not so..." he hesitated as if seeking the right word, his eyes moving down, settling on the same place as had Ramses, "affectionate." He smiled and patted the dog's head. "I must say Ramses, you have good taste. Under different circumstances, well..." he shrugged. He beamed as if what he said was an admiring compliment.

Beneath his aged exterior was a younger man, carnal, erotic, raw. His sexual magnetism channeled through the years so that he could shift his sexual energy into someone not fortitudinous and definitely not as imposing. Ruthless? He was the type who saw people as mere pawns on a chessboard. Easily maneuvered, or taken.

I wasn't sure he was the type to do the "dirty work." However, I was being held against my will. I had been drugged, kidnapped, and I was, without a doubt, in danger. One thing I was sure of, this man either killed Kenny or gave the order to have him killed.

"What do you want?"

"No, please. We can talk business over dinner." He began walking across the room toward the small cocktail bar. I was too terrified to move. Ramses still sat giving me his full attention.

"Ramses. Come here. Lie down."

The dog gave a happy yelp and trotted over to his master.

People say a person and his dog emulate each other. Cole and Ramses both were able to rapidly change dispositions.

I glanced at the door. Cole had his back to me. Ramses complied with the direct order and lay on the rug beside the fire. I was still dizzy from whatever I'd been drugged with, but I figured I might be able to outrun Cole. After all, he was older. But Ramses? With the right command, his attention could move from my feminine fragrances to the jugular in my neck.

I came around the chair. "Thanks, but I'm not hungry." I eased toward the door. This might be the only chance I'd get. I wasn't sure where I was, but being anywhere but inside this room seemed favorable to me.

Cole picked up one of the crystal decanters.

I made tiny shuffles closer to the door. I gave a glance at Ramses. He'd raised his head. But he wasn't necessarily paying attention to me, sniffing hungrily at whatever meal awaited.

I continued to creep.

Cole talked as he poured drinks. "King Ramses the second ruled for sixty-seven years."

Closer. Almost there.

I heard the dog yapping. I glanced back just as I was about to twist and make a dash for it. Cole stood to observe me, holding a glass in each hand. He must have seen that I'd moved, but he didn't threaten me. Instead, he walked over to the bust by the desk. He gazed at it, saying, "Most people recall Ramses' great military ability. History recognizes his **military genius** and his resilience in securing Egypt's borders from foreign invaders and fending off invasions from the Hittites and Nubians. His people considered him a god."

Did he think I wouldn't do it? That he could intimidate me like his dog? Again, I thought to twist around.

Ramses got to his feet.

Cole said, as if I was interested, "His rule was the second-longest in Egyptian history." He turned back to me. "Paintings generally depict him behind his war chariots. Like the paintings here." He lifted one of the glasses and indicated a nearby painting. "But the man's strength did not come from the men he left dead on the battlefield. Or the men he killed to survive as a ruler." He paused. He stood like a general before his troops, back straight, feet planted. "Do you want to know what truly made Ramses the great leader he was?"

I didn't give a rat's damn. Did this man see himself as a Ramses? I needed to wait for him to turn around again. Or for him to move over to the fireplace. That would take the dog's attention. Surely the possibility of a morsel from the table was more enticing than me.

He came over to where I stood, saying, "He found making peace with his enemies far more efficient." He handed me one of the cocktail glasses. Raised the one he held as if to make a toast. "To peace, Miss Dove, and our ability to come to a meeting of minds this evening." He smiled. He waited for me to lift my glass in a like salute.

"I don't drink," I informed him.

He took me by the elbow. "Come, Lillian. I am getting too old for war."

He'd called me Lillian, not Miss Dove. I felt he'd done it intentionally, his grip on my elbow less than gentle. "Have a drink. I won't tell anyone. We'll become friends. I only surround myself with friends." A threat? "I know you'll see your way to helping me."

He sat me in the chair facing the fireplace. He took the other facing the door. "Let's drink to our mutual well-being."

I'd lost any chance to escape. Would I get a second chance? I needed to put him off-guard. Let him think I was willing to listen to what he had to say. I set my glass on the table untouched.

He watched with amusement. "Maybe you'll be thirstier later." He raised his glass, saluted me without my joining in, and took a drink. He set the glass down and lifted off the lid of the tureen. He reached over toward me. I reared back. He chuckled. "Relax."

He picked up my soup bowl and ladled in soup, the redolent fragrance of basil coming off tomato bisque. After filling mine, he filled his. He took a spoonful, smiled. "I've found soup settling to the nerves," he said. Then he put down his spoon. He gazed at me as if he were asking a serious, thoughtful question. "Are you nervous, Lillian?"

I shook my head. I was probably trembling like a rabbit facing a wolf, but I wasn't about to give him the gratification of my admitting it. As cool and as innocently as I could, I returned, "What do you want?"

He leaned back in his chair. Smiled. "You have something that isn't yours by right. I want it back?"

"The flash drive?"

"Ah, I like a woman who gets right to the point."

"I don't have it. The police do."

His eyes jerked to the fireplace. His voice lost its amusement. "Yes, I'm aware the police have the drive you tossed into the water glass when you met with Liky. I've been notified eventually it may be readable, but if there is an image on it, I've also been assured it will be of bad quality and deemed unusable by law. Besides, I have made arrangements for its disposal."

He took up his glass, throwing what was left to the back of his throat. He frowned. "It was the first time you got in my way, Miss Dove. You shouldn't have met with him. You should choose your friends more wisely."

This came from a man who made friends by putting a gun to their heads. Fear shifted over slightly as I became annoyed at being given relationship advice. "Sounds like I did you a favor if the drive is ruined."

"I was told you were outspoken. I like that in a woman."

I bet. But, I did wonder who had given him personal information about me. Kenny?

"Under different circumstances, I think I'd like you. Maybe if you help me, I can find a place for you in my company."

"No thanks. While I may have faults, I do have a degree of integrity. I'd never work for someone like you."

He straightened. Frowned. Apparently, his appreciation for my candidness had its limits. A thin-lined grimace stretched on his lips. "Where is the drive Liky gave you?"

"You know where it is. It's with the police."

"I want the one he brought you here."

"Oh, you mean the memory card?"

The technicality appeared to ruffle him. His face hardened. No more Mr. Nice Guy.

I dared to go on. "If you know so much, then I don't need to tell you I only met with Kenny that once. I never saw him again until I saw him on my kitchen floor. Dead, if you aren't aware." As if. "I have no idea where a memory card is, Mr. Cole. Nor am I interested in finding it." No stopping me. "You've been badly informed." I stood up. "Kenny wasn't a friend of mine. He was Cressie's friend. Remember Cressie?"

What had this monster done to her?

His eyes widened. "Ah, yes, your friend." His tongue appeared slightly on his lips, and at that moment, I heard Stone's voice, *He took personal charge of making sure it was handled.*

"Sit down, Lillian."

I glanced over to Ramses, who seemed to have tired of the game and lulled into a nap. The door was directly behind me. If I could surprise both Cole and his dog, I might be able to make it out.

I made as if to sit back down. Then I twisted around. Knocked my chair away, crashing it to the floor. I didn't falter. I was sure at any moment Ramses was about to bury his teeth in my leg or pounce, knocking me to the ground, licking me to death.

I might not get another chance.

I couldn't risk turning back.

The door was so close. Almost within reach.

I stretched for the door handle. Grabbed it. Threw open the door.

Thompson.

I was saved.

CHAPTER THRITY-FIVE FIGHT BACK!

NOVEMBER 1ST, SATURDAY, AFTER 8 PM

I forced my eyes open. My hands were tied behind my back, my legs restrained. The room whirled like a beat-up, wobbly merry-go-round.

I rolled onto my side and vomited. The tang and gag of alcohol and bile sickened me.

I was in a small barn. The air held a hint of manure. Sacks were piled against the wall across from me. A wheelbarrow. A rake. Pitchfork. Bucket.

Where was I?

I shut my eyes to steady my swirling. It was cold. I was freezing. No, I was drunk. Hungover. I knew the chill.

I saw a slippery slope of failure in my future.

I was drunk, ruined, but alive. Was there hope?

An insight occurred to me. Of course, I was alive. Thompson couldn't kill me. Cole told him not to until I told him where the memory card was, and I couldn't have told him because I had no idea what Kenny had done with it.

Or had I? Did I make something up to get him to stop? When had he stopped? No memory of that. Nor any memory how I'd gotten here.

Another insight. If I'd lied in my drunken state, Cole wasn't a fool. He'd check out anything I said. I'd bet on it.

Get your wits about you, Lillian. Sober up.

First, how long had I been passed out? Hadn't someone said Cole was going to ship out the product at midnight. Was it Thompson who'd said it? Stone? Kelly? Did it matter who had said it? What time was it? If Cole didn't find the memory card, would he have me killed? If he did find it, would he kill me anyway?

I didn't want to hang around to find out.

The shed was dim. I lifted up as high as I could to get a better advantage. A lack of trained stomach muscles and another round of retching slumped me back onto my side.

I landed in what I'd already vomited.

I needed to move. If for no other reason than to have a clean empty space for another stomach attack. Wiggling got me nowhere but dizzier. I took a deep breath. My nose stung and felt swollen. My throat burned.

I pushed my shoes against the floorboard for traction, allowing me to move without too much wobble in a quarter circle turn. I could see shelves of garden products: weed killer, fertilizer, smaller tools for hand digging, colored jars. A garden shed. Not a barn. I was outside someone's home. Maybe somewhere with other houses close by.

I made another quarter turn. It was about all the farther I could go before another wretch of alcohol discharged. The wall I looked on now held ropes, chains. And beneath those, a riding lawnmower.

A sharp pain zinged me. It was so intense, my legs drew up without needing command. And then...oh, no. A horrible odor pillowed. I was going to be sick from both ends! The smell was disgusting/ Nauseated, I gagged. Retched.

Oh, no!

Embarrassing. Revolting. Served them right. Come in here now, Thompson. Take a good sniff!

Keep going, I encouraged myself. You need to get out. One more. One last turn. You can do it. I had to.

This time, I found the door.

Were they sending someone in to check on me? Thompson? Or were there others, too?

Thompson. I still had a hard time gripping onto the fact he worked for Cole. Did the Feds know of his deception? Did Cole have something he could hold over him bad enough that he would risk everything?

My mind revisited standing outside of Cressie's apartment. Thompson acted surprised when I mentioned the heroin I found planted on me. But, of course, he was the one who planted it. He hadn't figured I'd find it. It had to have been him. He was the only one who'd got close enough to me. But why the drug? And why the fake patrol officer? Of course, they were looking for the flash drive? Or maybe even then they knew about the card. But why not just kidnap me? Torture me then?

Unless Cole was hoping I'd fess up, knowing Kenny's scam, and thinking he could deal with me without the need for Thompson to give himself away. It would be handy for Cole to have someone buried within the Federal Bureau. Had he offered Thompson a position in the new company? A cushy office job? Enough money to retire on a sunny beach on an island no one would care about?

Thompson had made two calls. Did he call Cole to report to him that I'd got away and his men had been arrested?

The dots were beginning to connect. Thompson wouldn't know all my personal information. That's why he put my cell phone back in my car. He must have been at the station. Overhead Leveque saying he was going to release the car back to me. It would have been easy for him to go out into the lot and slip it in.

However, none of it mattered. Not the how or why. Not now. What was important at the moment was that I needed to escape.

The door was most surely locked, so no need to expend any effort trying to get to it. Besides, any and all movement turned my stomach. Caused posterior eruptions. And truly, did I have the strength to try to break down the door? If it was weakly structured, and I could, Thompson or someone like him would surely be close by, making all that effort worthless. I needed a better plan. I needed some way to protect myself.

I pushed backward a quarter turn. The lawnmower? I might be able to get my hands underneath the blades and cut away the tape. Find something on one of the shelves to use as a weapon. And if the mower started? It might be heavy enough to plow through the door.

I rolled onto my stomach. Actually, the position felt better. Scrunching up and lowering like an inchworm, I crawled across the floor. Sluggishly I slinked trying to quell the vomitous spew gagging my throat. I clenched, attempting to hold back the threatening toot from my backside.

My head ached. Temples throbbed. I began crying like a baby. Blubbering. I was so damn mad at myself for getting into this mess in the first place.

I inched and inched and inched, ignoring the smell, the pain to my knees, the wrench from the movement on my arms. I got closer and closer. Inch by inch by inch.

Bang.

A gunshot cracked. The sound came from outside. Close to the shed.

Another shot. Men's voices. It was hard to figure out what they were saying. However, I was fairly sure I recognized Thompson. And the other?

More gunshots. Shouting. More men.

I was being rescued.

CHAPTER THIRTY-SIX

A key turned in the lock. The shed door was thrown open. A person shoved in, stumbling and falling with a hard thump.

Leveque. His hands secured behind his back

Thompson torpedoed in after him. He grabbed Leveque, lifting him, and punched him on a jaw already showing red and bruising from other hits. "Who knows you're here?"

"Just me," Leveque spat blood. "I was looking for her."

Neither glanced over at me. I was still leaning flat on my stomach, head aimed for the lawnmower. I tried pushing myself in another turn, so as to hide where I'd been headed. Doing so, pushed me close to Leveque.

But Thompson didn't seem to care about me. "Won't matter," he gruffed. "We're almost out of here. Cole's decided to take both of you with the shipment. We'll let the cartel handle you. They're experts at disposal."

Leveque struggled to get up.

Thompson pulled back his boot and kicked Leveque in the head. The impact was so powerful, I heard a crack. Leveque's body weakened. His eyes closed. Blood oozed from his forehead.

Thompson leaned over and taped Leveque's legs.

Thompson regarded me. I wasn't sure what to expect. I was going to bite the hell out of him if he tried to carry me back into that room.

"It'll be all over soon, Lillian," he said.

He stepped over Leveque. Lowered himself next to me. "Cole figures with both you and Liky gone, the memory card may never surface. And if it does, he's got a nest of lawyers to fight any charges. Plus, the Feds' will be busy looking for Director Leveque's son." He laughed. "I'll be in the midst of all of it, handling most of the evidence."

"You won't get away with this." I sounded so cliché.

He sniffed. His expression soured. "What the hell is that smell?" He looked down to check to see if he'd stepped in something. "Disgusting." He wiped his boot clean on Leveque. "Guess you're not up for a goodbye drink."

He started barking laughter like the excited, vicious dog he was. He left the shed. The key in the lock turned.

"Leveque? Leveque? Can you hear me?"

I inched over closer to him.

His curly black hair was covered in blood. His face bruised. Had he been shot, too? Was he dead?

Inch, inch, inch, "Leveque?"

One eye opened. He saw me. He closed it.

"Are you all right?"

"Couldn't be better," he groaned, struggling. His face blanched as pain must have ripped through him

"Were you shot?"

"No, but I got one of theirs in the shoulder." He opened his eyes wider this time. "What the hell is that smell? Good God. Is someone dead in here?"

I didn't quite know what to say. So I said, "I'm not sure. I haven't been able to figure it out."

He struggled, this time rising slightly. He leaned toward me. Took a big sniff. "You!"

"It doesn't matter," I returned. "We need to get out of here. They'll kill us."

He lowered himself. Sighed. "Not a bad idea. It'd be nice if someone could stop you from getting into trouble." He sighed again. Struggled to get up. "They'll only shoot me or chop off my limbs before taking off my head. You'll get the worse of it. The men will…"

"Enough." Really, I didn't want to think about it. "I've got a plan."

"A plan?" He groaned. "Ah, sure. A plan."

"Yes, and a good one. Scoot over this way." I pushed myself backward a quarter way. Over here."

"Don't move. It stirs things up."

"Shut up. Look."

He had an easier time following my example. He didn't need to worm his way. Stronger, he merely got a good dig on the floor with his boot and spun.

"A lawnmower," I announced when he could see it. "We can cut the restraints with the blades unless you can get on your feet and knock down one of those tools." I nodded to the shelves.

No comment back from him. No, "Good plan, Lillian." No, "Thank you."

But he immediately began pushing himself over to the mower. Rolling on his side, he shoved his hands underneath, working the restraints against the blades. He grimaced several times, cutting himself in the process.

He pulled bloody hands out, freed. He sat up.

"How badly did you cut yourself?" I was concerned, but I couldn't keep veiled a triumphant cheer. My plan so far worked. We were getting out.

He untied his legs and struggled to get up on his feet. He groaned into a stand and steadied himself before moving to the shelves. Finding a tool, he came to me, flipped me on my side, and snipped the restraints. My arms were numb. Legs stiff. The movement sent out a painful reprisal of piercing electrical jolts.

Leveque gagged. "What'd they do to you? Smells like you're drunk and..."

He said "Smells like you're drunk" as if Thompson and I had a couple of social drinks together before he tied me up and tossed me inside.

I returned. "Cole, Thompson and I had a couple of drinks. To get to know each other better."

His eyebrow shot up.

"Don't be an idiot," I snarled, so wrongly accused. "They almost drowned me with alcohol. Cole wanted Thompson to find out where the memory card was hidden."

He still didn't look like he believed me. He sniffed, nodded, and positioned himself away from me, his attention moving from me to the shed door. "We need to get out of here. And fast."

"Do you think?" I asked sarcastically. "Where are we?"

"Not far from Dyer's."

Which didn't figure. The only house on the way out to Dyer's was just before Porch Bette's place. She got her name from her continual perch out on the front porch on a spring-broken, threadbare couch, no matter the season. Her place was a keystone. "Go out toward Porch Bette's, take a...."

"You're wrong. Porch Bette has dirt for a lawn. This isn't her gardening shed."

He scrunched his nose. Irritated. He moved farther away, and said, "You're right. It isn't. It's the person who lives directly behind her."

It took me a geographic moment. "Pane?"

He nodded.

That can't be right. "But, I was at Cole's. It was his furniture."

"Then they moved you."

Again, it didn't make sense. If they moved me, how did Leveque know where to find me? "How did you know I was here?"

"I didn't. Your mother called Dispatch and said you were trying to break into her place." He paused, "By the way..."

"Don't go there. We don't have time."

"Iver was with her."

Iver Dawson handled crime clean up. Not a specialty business. He was just licensed to handle things like blood and other toxic matter. He also worked at the hospital and Oaks Manor.

"He was there finishing cleaning the place. He said he saw you put your head over the wall, then fall. Heard you give a yell and thought you'd broken something. When he went to find out, he said he saw a big, bald guy carrying you over his shoulder, heading to a broken-down Honda."

"Thompson," I told him.

"Yeah. I figured that out." He rubbed his jaw. "Let's say we get out of here."

"Did you know it was Thompson before coming here? How'd you figure out he wasn't working undercover?"

It'd taken me too long to figure it out. Kidnapping me, keeping me from escaping Cole, I'd had to almost drown in booze to get it.

"The switch from his Harley to a broken-down Honda didn't make sense. Then, when the car was spotted here at Pane's, I couldn't figure out why he was here unless it meant you might be here, too."

"Did you see Cole?"

He shook his head. "Didn't need to. I put a call into Kelly. He's keeping an eye out on things at Dyer's." He explained, "Thompson was supposed to be keeping an eye on you."

"He was," I remarked.

"Yeah. Sorry. The only thing Kelly and I could come up with at first was that Thompson followed you here. That would have made sense if someone other than Thompson had been spotted carting you off.

"Eventually we put the pieces together. We should have figured this out way before.

"I notified Stone." He added, "When I came to take a closer look around, Thompson spotted me." He caught me up, "Cole's moving the shipment out earlier than they thought they would. Both Kelly and I think the reason's you."

"Cole said I was an obstacle to his success."

"Pain in the ass, if you ask me. Cole must have decided your disappearance would trigger a search. A search that would also blow Thompson's cover." He cocked his head. "Thompson has to be madder than hell at you. If it hadn't been for you, he might have got away with it."

He didn't wait for me to reply. He moved over to the shed door. Put his ear to it.

"Hear anything?"

He waved me quiet. I moved up next to him.

He pointed back where I'd been. "Stay away from me. As far as you can."

He started walking around, looking at the contents of the shed. I offered, hopefully, "If you told Kelly, he'll be coming for us."

"Dryer's first priority. Stone won't pull Kelly off of Dyer. And the clock's ticking. The agency's put too much money into this case to let everything go sour. Thanks to you, they have a kidnapping charge they can place on both Thompson and Cole. And if we can get out of here, they'll have two live victims for witnesses." He picked something off one of the shelves. Considered it. "They won't take the time to see how we're doing. Not yet. It'd be in our best interests to get out of here ourselves."

He crossed over, hefted the pitchfork. Picked up a sharp trowel and snugged it into his back pocket."

"I thought maybe if the lawnmower started?" I suggested.

He turned, stood to scrutinize the machine.

He made another round of the shed. Then he went back to the mower. Unscrewed the gas cap. Eyed the well. Replaced the cap. Going back over, he got hold of the pitchfork. He sat in the mower's seat, switched on the engine, and before I could ask him for the plan or what he wanted me to do, he roared off.

At first attempt, the mower bounced off the shed door. Leveque quickly switched the machine into reverse. Stomped on the gas pedal and made another run at it. On the second try, the door gave from the impact. Leveque rode out.

I ran out of the shed. Leveque jumped off the mower and immediately went for cover. I watched as he zig-zagged from bush to tree toward Councilman Pane's two-story Georgian unimpeded.

CHAPTER THIRTY-SEVEN
BELIEVE IN YOU

NOVEMBER 1ST, SATURDAY, 60 MINUTES TO SHIPMENT

Leveque broke into the house. It was empty. Councilman Pane had an invalid wife, yet, no one seemed to be home. Her or her nurse.

He went to get his car. He said he parked one of the patrol cars off-road where it couldn't be seen from the house. He came back, "Four flat tires."

He went back to the house to find a phone. While he did, I walked around, thinking I couldn't have been here. All the furniture was very traditional. Pictures of their kids and grandchildren were found in most of the rooms.

Cole's place mirrored his narcissism.

Upstairs I found a room with a hospital bed. His wife's? A Jack-in-Jill bathroom connected to what must have been the nurse's room. Another bedroom, male. And one more, what must have been a guest room.

No sign of Cole. I went back downstairs.

"I've called in," Leveque said. "Miner's on his way."

"I couldn't have been here, Leveque," I told him, still confused. "The room I was in was completely different in style."

He moved in the opposite direction where I'd come. "I think I found where they had you."

I followed him through the dining room, kitchen, a small hallway and what appeared to be a new addition. The architecture on the outside of the house gave no hint to having been added on to.

He opened a door. The sharp whiff of alcohol hit me. The room was a huge departure from the other parts of the house. Pane may have added the room at some point to give himself a private area to do council business, but Cole had taken over. There was the table over by the fireplace. Cole's desk. The statue of Ramses.

Ramses. The statue's projected superior countenance glaring out over the room maddened me. Enraged me to a point where I ran over to the table and knocked everything off on the floor. Tipped over the chairs. Ran to the small bar, clouting off bottles, shards of glass flying to the floor.

"Lillian, what the hell?"

I flew over to Ramses. Looked him right in the eye. "Peace isn't negotiating a pact with an enemy to promote egotistical, immoral greed," I screamed.

I grabbed ahold of the bust. Thompson's smug shiny, bald head. The thought was to smash it to the floor as if it was Cole's head in my hands. For Thompson's two-timing, double-crossing torture.

The bust was massive. My grip too small.

I ran from the statue to the cabinet and taking the small statues and figurines out, I threw them across the room. Knocking off heads. Shattering them.

Leveque grabbed me. "Knock it off."

"I want to kill them." My voice held a note of hysteria.

"I'm sure you do. But you're destroying evidence. Now get a grip."

Mitch Miner entered the room, gun drawn. "Everything okay in here?"

Leveque released me. "I need to get out to Dyer's, stat."

Miner glanced from Leveque to me. "The Chief and the Feds are there," Miner informed him.

"And Agent Thompson?" Leveque asked.

"I saw him coming up the road when I was coming down here."

"Damn, let's go." Leveque moved quickly.

Miner said, "You're hurt."

Leveque brushed his forehead with his hand and brought back blood. "Scratch. I'm fine."

"What's that odor?" Miner sniffed.

Leveque nodded over to me. "Don't get too close. They did a number on her."

Leveque started out, Miner followed. So did I.

"You stay here," Leveque ordered. "Miner can take me to Dyer's and then come back and get you to the hospital."

"I'm fine. I don't need to get to the hospital."

"I said, you're staying here. This isn't a game. It's too dangerous."

"Look, Leveque. I've been kidnapped. Tortured. I'm not staying here."

"Come on, Miner. She's staying." He jogged over to the patrol car.

"I'll come back as soon as I can," Miner said.

Both men got in the patrol car and drove toward Dyer's.

Kelly knew about Thompson. He'd stop him. Unless Kelly was also...

I stared at the shed where I'd been kept. Setting it on fire wasn't beyond my thoughts. I twisted around. Pane's house could use a good smokin' too. I wasn't about to go back inside and wait. What if hearing that his shipments were being stopped, Cole came back to hide at Pane's?

I wanted to go back upstairs and take a shower. I stripped, throwing my underwear in the bushes. Shook out my jeans as best I could and tugged them back on.

Better? Of course, I could no longer smell myself.

I went over to the lawnmower. Leveque left the keys in the ignition. I started up the machine and headed down the road at a rate of maybe fifteen, twenty miles an hour.

Cole killed Cressie. He'd killed Kenny. He would have had me killed, too. If anyone deserved to be at the action when his operation was stopped, it was me.

Miner returned before I got more than a mile. "What the hell are you doing, Lillian?"

I got off the mower. I hurried over to the car and got in on the passenger side. "Let's go."

"I'm going to catch hell for this."

"You're going to catch hell right now if you don't put some lead into it."

CHAPTER THIRTY-EIGHT

M iner veered off the main road, short of coming up on Dyer's Moving and Storage. A couple of unharvested cornfields separated a farmer's barn from the building. FPD and unmarked SUV's, probably Feds, were parked in the lot. I saw Leveque standing over by Agent Stone, Chief Kaefring, and Lieutenant Manville.

I glanced around, looking for Thompson. Did his absence mean he'd been arrested?

I knew if Charles or Leveque spotted me, they'd ship me straight out. Whereas, Stone would probably stake me out in the cornfield hoping to tempt Cole. It was best to keep as low a profile as I could. I walked over to the open barn door where a group of officers stood waiting for instructions.

"What's happening?" I asked Sergeant Wheeler.

"What're you doing here? I thought Miner left to take you to the hospital."

"I don't need to go to the hospital. I'm fine."

He eyed me. But he didn't remark on any nasty smells. Maybe I'd air-cleaned on the mower.

"Miner," Wheeler called out. "Get her out of here."

Miner came over. Gave me a disgruntled look. "Easier said than done."

I asked Wheeler. "Have any of the trucks left? Is Dyer in on this, too?"

"As far as we know, Dyer's thinking he's landed a big contract."

I wasn't so sure. We both may have said the same about Councilman Pane.

"Those guys over there." He nodded to men dressed in black swat gear, carrying powerful guns. "Those are Feds. NEA and FBI. See the guy talking to the Chief? He's FBI Director of the Chicago office."

"Yeah. We've met," I told him.

"You've met?"

Suddenly, Garth Davis, standing a few feet away, dropped to the ground.

CHAPTER THIRTY-NINE

A nother shot. Then another.

Guns were pulled. Shouting.

What was going on? I glanced around, not understanding the reason for the gunfire until I saw men similarly protected and armed move out from the edge of the cornfield. It was an ambush. Someone had tipped Cole's people off.

Bullets popped. Whizzed.

Like I'd been picked up by a whirlwind, I was carried then hurled inside the barn. Sergeant Wheeler and Miner jumped in behind me closing the barn door.

"Get back," Miner yelled. "Find cover."

I backed away from the opening. It was a small barn with two stalls, hay covering the floor, and two, paned, dirty windows. Seeing a bag of seed hanging from a pulley, as if the farmer had wrenched it from a truck bed, been called away, and thought to store it later, I scurried around it, holding it as a shield.

Wayward bullets thumped the barn.

Both men had guns drawn. Wheeler yelled to Miner. "Garth's moving. We need to get him. I'll cover."

Miner nodded. Wheeler stationed himself in the door's opening. Miner, stood behind him, waiting for Wheeler to give the order. Wheeler shouted, "Go." Wheeler began shooting without stopping.

I thought it was the last time I'd see Mitch Miner.

"What's going on?" I shouted to Wheeler. "Is he okay?"

He'd probably been gone merely seconds, but it didn't feel as if time was continuing. It was as if this moment held all there was, as if it would never end.

Then Miner was back, rushing in backward, dragging Garth by his vest strap. "Got him."

"Get him stable," Wheeler said, not taking his eyes from outside. "Then get back over here."

Miner dragged him into one of the stalls well beyond the barn door. He said to me, "We need something to stop the bleeding."

I saw the rags. Clean or not, they'd have to do. "Here." I grabbed the rags, ran over and squatted next to Garth. "Go on. I'll take care of him."

Miner didn't argue. He raced back over to Wheeler.

"Garth, can you hear me?" His face was colorless. He'd had no warning what was about to happen to him. His gun was still in his holster.

I lifted an eyelid. His eye stared back at me. I didn't know what I was looking for, but I thought I spotted a flick of motion from his pupil, from the sudden change of light.

I needed to find where he'd been shot. The protective vest was designed to protect his heart and lungs. He was bleeding where his vest stopped.

"You're going to be okay." I removed his gun and belt. I unhooked his vest. Once off, I was able to see the blood was coming from his right shoulder, just below his collarbone. A large hole, open, red, pumping blood. Small, white bone fragments. I tore his shirt, ripped again to get some good material, then placed it over the open wound and pressed down.

The harder I applied pressure, the more blood seemed to puddle around him. I abandoned the pressure long enough to flip him onto his side. The bullet had gone straight through.

The assault outside continued. Explosions. Continuous reports from automatics.

"We're outnumbered," Miner shouted to Wheeler.

"Richards's down," Wheeler shouted back.

From their alarmed voices, it sounded like the defending battle being waged outside was failing.

Wheeler hurried over to where I'd just finished securing pressure to both of Garth's wounds. "You okay?"

"We're both fine." My voice may have sounded calm and sure, but I was a trembling inside.

"Good. Miner and I need to get out of here and add our support." He put two fingers to Garth's neck. "He's lost a lot of blood, but I think he's going to be all right."

"As soon as we're gone," he ordered, "barricade this door. Don't let anyone in unless you're sure who it is."

I nodded. Heard a groan. Gath was gaining consciousness.

Wheeler went back over to the door. Both he and Miner took heed, before running out.

A shot pierced the barn siding, cracking wood, and whizzed so close, I felt its gust of wind.

Pulling Garth to his good side, I lugged him farther back into the stall for more protection. I packed hay up around him to keep him warm. Found a horse's blanket and laid it over him.

He moaned. His eyes fluttered open, then closed.

Rookie cop. Newly married. Only this time, his wife wasn't going to get the call she daily feared. He was going to live.

But how many more were hurt? Wheeler said Richards was down. And Charles? Was he all right?

The pandemonium continued to rage. Bullets broke through the siding, zinged across the barn. I knew I had to secure the barn door, but how? The door opened out, not in. How could I barricade it? I glanced around, seeing the feeding bag on the pulley.

Finding a knife, dull but useable, I got a ladder and climbed up to where the rope hooked the bag. I cut through the bags burlap, seeds spewing out into a clattering pile on the floor. I looked around again. Found a piece of wood I thought would do the trick.

I went over to the barn doors. Each door offered a handhold. I slipped the wood between them, making the door hard to open. And to make sure, I hooked the rope in the middle of the wood. I pulled making the rope taut, tied it to a post. I surveyed my work. It was the best I could do.

Then I went back to Garth making him as comfortable as I could. "Hang on, it's just a flesh wound. You'll get some of that time off Mary Beth's been asking you to take."

His eyes fluttered. Was he letting me know he could hear me? He winced. Groaned.

Then, I felt something behind me.

A breeze? A stirring.

Close.

"Don't move."

CHAPTER FORTY

S weat ran down his face. Blood streaked his vest and clothes. His or someone else's?

I glanced over to the barn door. It was as I'd left it. "How'd you get in here?"

"No time for that," Thompson snarled. "Get up."

He aimed his gun at Garth. I stepped in the gun's path. "Don't trouble yourself, he's not going to make it anyway."

He didn't move the gun's aim, straight at me.

My knees trembled. I prayed it didn't show. I didn't want to give Thompson the satisfaction. I wasn't afraid, as much as I was livid with hate for what he'd done to me. It wasn't just the booze he'd poured down my throat, strangling me to a point I'd lost consciousness. It was destroying the five years I'd achieved opening a new life. A life without a booze rattled brain.

Was this how Cressie felt when she saw Cole? Was she afraid? Or was she infuriated like I was? Did she know her death was because of Kenny?

"You should have run when you had the chance," he said. "None of this would have happened if you had just given up the card."

I took a gamble. "Kill me, and Cole will never find it."

"Killing you would be too kind. Cole still wants the card. I may not have got where it is out of you, but our friends across the border will." He offered a wicked grin.

"You'll never get away with this." I glanced at the barn door again. How did he get in?

He laughed maliciously. A nasty, crazy cackle. His eyes glanced around the room wildly, as if he was worried about what I was saying might come real. A federal agent sentenced to prison for turning against his own? He'd get back five hundred times what he'd forced on me.

I almost grinned.

"You're right," he suddenly agreed. He lifted the gun. "What do I care if Cole gets his or not? I'm getting out of here as soon as the shipments are gone."

Something beyond him caught my notice. A quick movement of shadow. I needed to keep him talking.

"You're not thinking, Thompson," I said."Even if the shipment gets out of here, the trucks'll be stopped. It'll take hours to get to the Mexican border."

He suddenly jerked his head. Listened. Raised his arm, moving the gun higher. This time pointing it directly at my head.

"Cole's smart. He's got it all planned." He seemed amused by my lack of gangster-thinking-ability. "None of the other shipments have the product. They're dummies. The Feds will be following those. Stone didn't know about this transfer until a couple of days ago. Besides, Cole has other means of getting it to the border."

His body flinched. "That you, Kelly?" he shouted.

No answer. Kelly? Was Kelly on the other side working for Cole, too?

Another noise, the shuffling of feet on floorboards coming from the post where I'd tied the rope. Had Kelly came in the same way Thompson had?

"Take one more step and she's dead."

Then Kelly wasn't working for Cole.

His threat unnerved me. While Thompson talked about getting away, he had to know he wasn't going to get out of this alive, either. I might not have gangster-think, but I was smart enough to know people like Cole didn't like to leave loose ends. Isn't that how Thompson had put it to me when talking about me? Only, I wasn't the only loose end here. Thompson was also a dangling thread needing to be snipped.

Snap. Another sound.

Thompson's eyes widened. His head moved slightly as if he was readying to turn around and defend himself.

His head exploded before the report of the gun echoed. His body remained standing, his hand still aimed at me.

I twisted, scuttling to find protection. But I couldn't get away fast enough. Not before Thompson's body fell, crashing down in dead weight, knocking me to the ground with him.

I panicked, hysterical. "Get off. Get off." Kicking. "Help." Struggling from beneath him, I felt sure whoever killed Thompson would be after me next. As if at any moment, a gun would be put to my head.

Even when he was pulled off, I didn't stop screaming for help. Surely someone would hear me. Miner? Wheeler? They knew I was inside with Garth.

Nor did I stop when hands pulled me away from Thompson's dead body. Lifted me up and away.

"You're okay. It's over." Words whispered to me.

I saw the barn door open. Men in gear began running in. Several ran over to Garth.

"Get the paramedics in here. Officer down."

But still, I couldn't stop the fury that had gripped me. I began hitting the person holding me. Striking his face. Pulling his hair.

He wrapped his arms tighter around me.

"She okay?" someone asked.

Charles?

"Yeah. Peachy." The voice holding me answered.

My heart thumped against my ribs. My body tense.. Eventually, I realized I was out of danger.

As my storm weakened, so did his hold.

A dirty, sweaty face, dark brown eyes, and dark brown curls smashed wet with blood stood above me.

Leveque.

The heat of anger reboiled, exploding. "You could have killed me," I yelled.

He scoffed. "Don't think the idea didn't cross my mind."

CHAPTER FORTY-ONE   PROVEN INNOCENT

NOVEMBER 1ST, SATURDAY, AFTER MIDNIGHT

I hate hospitals, especially the emergency ward.

Nurses and doctors responded to the wounded men as soon as the doors pulled open. IV bags hung from gurneys. Curtained rooms offered standing room only. Voices hinted of a panic all of us felt. Only as with emergencies, everyone maneuvered with trained effectiveness.

Charles insisted I get checked out, although, I didn't consider myself hurt. Bruised, emotionally degraded, yes, but thanks to Miner for shoving me into the barn, I escaped a wayward bullet. And one directly aimed at me. Thompson would have had me in his sights. His coming into the barn showed his desperation. Not in being caught. His arrest was inevitable. Evidence would show his deceit and connection.

His need to hurt me had become personal.

Thompson killed Kenny. Not a solution Cole sanctioned. But, Thompson couldn't hold back his anger. It wasn't that Kenny wouldn't give away where the card was located, Thompson's rage and fear of being caught must have volcanically erupted. Kenny wasn't playing the game by Cole and Thompson's rules.

Neither was I. That was the rub.

The doctor gave me a prescription for Xanax and suggested I go home and get some rest. I didn't leave immediately. I found out where Garth had been taken.

The first to arrive at the hospital, he'd been treated and given a room. Miner stood in the hallway, leaning against the wall, his eyes closed. Exhausted. Too tired to go anywhere.

"Is Garth okay?" I kept my voice down not wanting to disturb those inside Garth's room, or Miner if he'd truly fallen asleep standing up.

He opened an eye. "Lillian. You okay?" Both eyes came open. "Have you seen a doctor, yet?"

I showed him my bottle of Xanax. "I'm fine."

Actually, I didn't know how I was. Physically my body hurt as if I'd been put in a container and rolled down a hill. Every muscle screamed. Emotionally? I guess I was in shock. My voice sounded robotic.

"I could use a couple of those myself, but I've got to get back. Evidence techs are on the scene. Three different divisions. Three investigations. There's going to be a mound of paperwork."

"But they got Cole?" I wanted it confirmed. Knowing he'd been arrested vindicated Cressie's death. Kenny's. My safety.

He nodded. "From what Wheeler told me, they caught him hiding inside one of the trucks. I guess he was hoping to make an escape after everything settled down and before the vehicles were searched."

"Coward after all," I said, thinking back to his Ramses comparison.

Miner gave me the good news that Garth's collarbone had been fractured by the bullet and, of course, he'd lost blood, but he was going to be all right." He reached out, placing his hand on my shoulder. "The news might have been different if you hadn't known what to do."

I wanted to say something witty like I've watched a lot of medical shows on television, but this was not the time for humor. Garth lying in his hospital bed, pale, machines beeping, Mary Beth at his bedside, crying, didn't lend for a jovial mood.

"How about Richards?" I asked.

"He's in surgery, but the doctors say he's not critical. He should recover." He rubbed his forehead, his eyes closed. While unhurt, he, too, was emotionally drained. It could have very well been him in a hospital room. I wondered if he'd called his wife yet to tell her that he was all right. Because by sun up, the news media would be all over town. Frytown would be again glued to their televisions or on their phones.

He pulled away from the wall. "Four of ours hurt. An NEA agent killed."

"Do you know who?" Of course, I thought of Kelly.

He shook his head. "I've been here."

"Thanks, Miner," I said.

"For what?"

"If you hadn't pushed me inside the barn, I might have been taking up a room, or a body added to the morgue."

"From what I heard, the Feds set you up as a guinea pig."

"Of sorts," I agreed. "I missed figuring out who was hoping to catch me, however."

"Meaning?"

"Thompson. I didn't realize he was dirty until I saw him with Cole."

He put both of his hands on my shoulders. Squeezed. "Quit being so hard on yourself." He smiled. "You did a good job, Lillian."

Our conversation began to falter. In a couple of days, what happened would rule all conversations

I left the hospital wondering what decided our fate.

CHAPTER FORTY-TWO

I had one of the officers drop me off at Clarence's house. By the time I unlocked the door and went inside, my feet only moved because I commanded them to do so. The thought of sleeping on a make-shift bed in the living room wasn't a consideration. I grabbed the covers and pillow and made my way to Clarence's bed. I took a long, hot shower. It felt great to be clean. The Xanax stayed unopened. I didn't need it. I was so exhausted, I think I must have fallen asleep before getting in bed.

CHAPTER FORTY-THREE

I jarred awake. Twisted and squirmed as if my hands and legs were still tied. It took a moment or two for me to realize I wasn't still lying on the floor in the shed. I was in bed. Safe.

Someone was knocking on the front door.

"Just a minute."

I found an old robe of Clarence's in his closet. Checking out the window, I saw the cruiser in the driveway. I opened the door and fell into Charles's arms.

"Shhhh, you're okay, now." He held me, his arms holding me tight. "It's all over."

Emotional waves rippled through me. I wept as if I'd been told someone died. With each sob, he pulled me closer.

He led me inside, not releasing his hold. "Lillian, you're all right. You're going to be okay."

I heard the catch in his voice, his exhaustion and anxiety releasing before his lips found mine. "You're safe," he repeated, kissing my face. "It's over," he whispered, finding my lips waiting for his.

I took his hand and led him to the bedroom. He pulled off my robe, stroking me calm, quieting my sobs. Our eyes held the only conversation, words were too arduous. Or maybe there were no words for what we both felt.

Touch triumphed. His hands cupped my face, moved over my body, touching me, exploring, before he found his way back. "Lillian."

We depleted each other.

He lay on his side, his eyes still holding mine while we both fell asleep. When I woke again, he was gone.

I might have thought it all a dream if he hadn't left his hat, lying on the sofa, where it'd been tossed.

CHAPTER FORTY-FOUR

I found some coffee in a cupboard. Taking a steaming cup, I went into the living room and curled up on the couch. I turned on the television and switched to KETV News. It was a new day, tomorrow had arrived, but I didn't have a clue what to do with it.

I was shocked to learn it wasn't Sunday, as I'd expected, but Monday.

Bobby Bowen was standing in front of the police station. I turned up the volume. "What has occurred here in this small city is unprecedented. Federal, State, County, and local police are still reeling from an investigation moving across several states and crossing international borders.

"Acting Mayor Morton Dyer, his company caught up in this criminal inquiry, is a witness to Axel Cole's felonious actions. He is also witness to Mayor John Otis's bigamy scandal."

The camera pulled wide. Morton Dyer, in his fifties, tall, wearing a raincoat on a day threatening showers, stood next to Bobby Bowen, along with this wife, Liz.

"I've been told any charges for you personally have been dropped"

Dyer nodded. "I was never charged. I was contacted by the FBI and I fully cooperated." He gave a nervous stammer. "I had no idea what was being transported."

"But," Bobby interrupted. "From a reputable source, I've been told it was you who informed the police about Councilman Andrew Pane. Who has been charged with several counts of aiding and abetting a felonious act."

Dyer nodded.

Bowen moved the microphone to Liz Dyer. "You, Mrs. Dyer, contacted Jessica Feldman?"

Liz seemed distraught. She hung onto her husband's arm. "I had to," she said, looking directly into the cameras. "When I was in Baxter visiting my mother's ill sister, I saw Mayor Otis and that woman. I couldn't let him get away with doing that to Corabelle. Or his children. I did what any other person would have done in my place." She heaved a sigh. "Really. This was someone I've known most of my life. I couldn't believe it." She asked Bowen, "Where were his moral values?"

Bowen didn't seem to have any answers for her. He asked Morton Dyer about taking over as mayor.

"The council have asked me to take over as acting mayor. Once officially elected, I will do my best to re-establish the reputation of Frytown as being a city where its streets and its people can live safely and with integrity."

I turned off the television. What had happened to the mayor would be told and retold for days to come.

I picked up Charles's cap. Had he left it here intentionally? Was this a new beginning for both of us?

CHAPTER FORTY-FIVE
NOVEMBER 4TH, WEDNESDAY

It'd rained the last couple of days, steadily. Today, a sweet scent moved through the air promising spring, not winter. Yet, spring was still far, far away. And the weather forecasters continued to promise a white Thanksgiving.

I hadn't left Clarence's house. Even though I had taken over his room, it's how I still saw it: Clarence's house. Dahlia's condo. Me, homeless.

I closed the bedroom window. While trying to motivate myself to see the day differently, I hadn't woken up before noon. But I took the clearing of the skies this morning as a sign for me to get back into life. I couldn't hide forever.

Yet, that's what I wanted to do. Stay inside forever.

I dreamed of Axel Cole's room in the Pane house. Some nights the dream started with cowering behind a chair in the corner of the room. My body quivering with each soft slide crossing the carpet as if whatever was perusing me slithered like a snake.

All dreams ended with me in front of a fireplace, a bottle of Absolut in my hands, my mouth greedy, letting the ice-cold liquor slip between my lips, numbing them, frozen, numbing me so I couldn't move. I didn't want to have to move ever again.

I would wake up screaming, the sensation of drowning overwhelming my sweaty body. The sheets drenched. Covers in a tangle or thrown to the floor. The taste of vodka filling my throat.

When someone knocked on the door, I thought it was Charles. I hadn't seen him since he'd come that first night. Only, when I opened the door, it wasn't him.

"You're looking good." Leveque scanned my appearance.

Hair pulled back into a ponytail, I was wearing a pair of Clarence's pants, legs rolled, and a shirt of his. The clothes still carried a faint scent of his pipe tobacco.

"What do you want, Leveque?"

"I need you to do something about your mother."

"What about my mother?"

"She's been calling three, four times a day wondering where you are."

"I called and told Nelly Crow where I was if there was an emergency. My mother's on her own now."

Nelly told me Dahlia was still living in the condo. I needed to go and get my things, I couldn't wear Clarence's clothes forever, but going would mean a battle.

Quite frankly, I was too damn tired and defeated to battle Dahlia.

"Well somebody needs to do something." His cheek twitched. "There's no getting a word in once she's on the phone."

"Look, Leveque," I started to close the door. "She's not my problem."

He said, "Last call, she wanted to know how to call animal control. She said she had a cat she needed to get rid of."

Bacardi. I'd abandoned him. Guilt flushed over me.

He said, "Look. Do me this favor. See if you can get her to quit calling the station."

I didn't owe him a favor, but Bacardi?

He glanced inside. "You're lucky. This is a pretty nice place."

I changed the subject. "What's happening with Cole?"

"Fed's got him now. Stone's taking credit for the bust."

"Come on," I'll take you.

"I've got my own car." I looked to the driveway. Empty.

"Percy had it picked up. Said it needed new tires."

Percy? It took too much effort to argue. "Okay, take me to my car. I need to get some of my things, anyway. But, Dahlia never listens to me."

CHAPTER FORTY-SIX

H e turned in the opposite direction from where he should have on Church Street.

"Where are we going?"

"I thought you might want to check Discount."

My stomach stirred. I wasn't ready to face the ruin, yet.

"Just take me to get my car."

We turned onto Lakeside Road. Discount was located on the next corner. There were patrol cars parked outside.

"What's going on?"

"Hell if I know," Leveque said, pulling up slightly on the steering wheel to get a better look himself. "There must have been another break-in."

"No!"

He pulled behind Dick Cooney's car. I opened the door and got out. I saw Percy's truck in the parking lot. Beside it, the Mustang.

Mitch Miner stood on the porch. Out of uniform. He was talking to Percy, arm still in a sling. Pete came out, holding a broom. Others inside began filling the doorway.

"I don't understand," I said, not moving. They were all standing smiling like they held a secret.

"Come on," Leveque said. He gave me a push.

The group on the porch parted as we walked up. The floor of the store was clean. The racks filled fully.

Donna stood behind the counter. "Surprise!" she shouted.

The shelves behind her were also completely stocked.

"How did you?"

She chuckled devilishly. "We fooled you, didn't we?" Her rhinestone glasses twinkled along with her eyes.

"I can't afford to pay for this."

I still wasn't getting it. I thought she'd ordered more inventory.

"I'll be your first customer," Percy said, holding up a six-pack he'd pulled out of the cooler.

"I think we should celebrate." Someone else shouted.

It was Garth Davis. looking still pale, but smiling. Mary Beth stood by his side, holding a bottle of champagne.

Miner came over to me, maybe noticing my confusion, unbelieving anyone would do something this nice for me. Ever.

"I had Donna check out your insurance on this place," he explained. "Found out you didn't have insurance."

"I hadn't managed to get to it, yet."

"That's what we figured. So everyone in the station pitched in to put you back in business."

Beer was opened and passed around. They were all off duty. Garth couldn't have any of the bubbly because he was on pain meds, but Mary Beth had a glass or two."

I went behind the counter.

"You okay, Sweetie?" Donna asked. Her eyebrow lifting high above her glasses' frame.

I looked at the bottle of Absolut on the shelf. Just seeing the bottle caused my mouth to salivate. Pavlov's dog, I thought. My new friends may be trying to give me back my life, but Cole may have taken away all I'd worked for.

I licked my lips.

Go ahead. Celebrate.

Then I heard Cressie's voice. *One tequila, two tequila, three tequila, floor.*

Eventually, everyone left. It was just Leveque and I. He sat on the counter grinning down at me. "Surprised you, didn't we?"

Tears came. I didn't cry when I walked in seeing what they had all done, but alone, looking around, seeing that the store was almost in the same condition as it was when I left Wednesday night, gave me such a great feeling of being loved, I could do nothing else but weep.

Leveque leaped down off the counter. "Hey, I hope those are happy tears."

CHAPTER FORTY-SEVEN

H e turned in the opposite direction from where he should have on Church Street.

"Where are we going?"

"I thought you might want to check Discount."

My stomach stirred. I wasn't ready to face the ruin, yet.

"Just take me to get my car."

We turned onto Lakeside Road. Discount was located on the next corner. There were patrol cars parked outside.

"What's going on?"

"Hell if I know," Leveque said, pulling up slightly on the steering wheel to get a better look himself. "There must have been another break-in."

"No!"

He pulled behind Dick Cooney's car. I opened the door and got out. I saw Percy's truck in the parking lot. Beside it, the Mustang.

Mitch Miner stood on the porch. Out of uniform. He was talking to Percy, arm still in a sling. Pete came out, holding a broom. Others inside began filling the doorway.

"I don't understand," I said, not moving. They were all standing smiling like they held a secret.

"Come on," Leveque said. He gave me a push.

The group on the porch parted as we walked up. The floor of the store was clean. The racks filled fully.

Donna stood behind the counter. "Surprise!" she shouted.

The shelves behind her were also completely stocked.

"How did you?"

She chuckled devilishly. "We fooled you, didn't we?" Her rhinestone glasses twinkled along with her eyes.

"I can't afford to pay for this."

I still wasn't getting it. I thought she'd ordered more inventory.

"I'll be your first customer," Percy said, holding up a six-pack he'd pulled out of the cooler.

"I think we should celebrate." Someone else shouted.

It was Garth Davis. looking still pale, but smiling. Mary Beth stood by his side, holding a bottle of champagne.

Miner came over to me, maybe noticing my confusion, unbelieving anyone would do something this nice for me. Ever.

"I had Donna check out your insurance on this place," he explained. "Found out you didn't have insurance."

"I hadn't managed to get to it, yet."

"That's what we figured. So everyone in the station pitched in to put you back in business."

Beer was opened and passed around. They were all off duty. Garth couldn't have any of the bubbly because he was on pain meds, but Mary Beth had a glass or two."

I went behind the counter.

"You okay, Sweetie?" Donna asked. Her eyebrow lifting high above her glasses' frame.

I looked at the bottle of Absolut on the shelf. Just seeing the bottle caused my mouth to salivate. Pavlov's dog, I thought. My new friends may be trying to give me back my life, but Cole may have taken away all I'd worked for.

I licked my lips.

Go ahead. Celebrate.

Then I heard Cressie's voice. *One tequila, two tequila, three tequila, floor.*

Eventually, everyone left. It was just Leveque and I. He sat on the counter grinning down at me. "Surprised you, didn't we?"

Tears came. I didn't cry when I walked in seeing what they had all done, but alone, looking around, seeing that the store was almost in the same condition as it was when I left Wednesday night, gave me such a great feeling of being loved, I could do nothing else but weep.

Leveque leaped down off the counter. "Hey, I hope those are happy tears."

CHAPTER FORTY-EIGHT
SUPPOSE

Suppose there are reasons for the road we take.

The choices we make.

The pain, happiness, and love we feel.

Suppose everything touches everything.

There is no separation.

If I **suppose** this is true, then I see no path is narrow,

no road taken straight.

If I **suppose**, then I can see beginnings are endings,

and endings are never quite complete.

-Lillian June Dove

www.ingramcontent.com/pod-product-compliance
Lightning Source LLC
Chambersburg PA
CBHW020954180626
46814CB00003B/1084